A Book for a Cunt.

Some people should be dipped in vagisil, then they wouldn't be such irritating twats.

Christmas Gifts

A collection of short stories by aspiring new writers.

Foreword.

On Tuesday nights, in the windy seaside resort of Cleethorpes, a ragtag group of writers gather to inspire and motivate each other into producing short stories and poems each week. This anthology is a collection of Christmas-themed works by these authors. We all hope you enjoy reading them as much as we enjoyed writing them. In fact, we hope you enjoy reading them more, because some of found it a chore!

A Christmas Poem.

By Andrew Leake

When I think of Christmas

I think of when it meant something dear to me

Nowadays as the month of December approaches I feel nothing at all

Despite my kids meaning the world to me.

I remember how my Mother's food smelt and how my Dad would tell jokes

Around the table that was set for 4

My little sister laughing loudly; I ate so much I almost emptied the contents on the floor

The presents meant nothing to me, and it was not like there were many underneath the tree

What meant the most is seeing my Dad's and Mother's faces when they sat closely by

They were in love and they were in love with me.

My sister by my side I reached out and grabbed her hand

I loved her with all my might and wished this moment would never end.

My family meant the world, and I was just a kid back then

Playing cards, chess, darts and quizzes were the rage and there were no gadgets to rid us of our youth

Nowadays kids gawp at their screens but hardly see what's going on around them

I feel sorry for them whilst they feel nothing at all.

Before the meal we used to connect our hands and prayed to God for forgiveness

I remember it all like it was yesterday

Now I sit with my wife and kids

And try to remember the magic of it all

And yet it is now me who feels nothing

I thought Christmas was sacred and all

But it's not, and it never was

What made it special was the family spirit that my family fostered

And so, I wish everyone a Merry Christmas

And hope you've sent out your cards to the relatives and friends close to your hearts

I hope you've hugged or rang your grandparents and let them know how much you've missed them

I hope that you all have a lovely time

And if the presents you receive aren't to your taste try to remember that some celebrate Christmas out in the cold

Without any loved ones by their sides they get abused and are led astray

Some don't even have a coat to protect them from the elements

I'm lucky to have this feast in front of me.

As the Christmas Carols ring out on Christmas Day

Remember that we are all united

By the spirit we foster

Inside of us all.

Snow Day.

By Gemma Owen-Kendall

This was the first time Owen and Edward had ever seen snow, they'd seen it on many festive films but never outside their bedroom window. It was an early Saturday morning in December when both boys woke up to everywhere outside looking so white. A wintry blizzard had visited the town of Grimsby over-night and continued into the early hours of the morning, snowflakes fluttered thick and heavy.

'Mummy. Daddy, come quick. It is snowing' Called out Edward.

In their half asleep state both parents entered the young boys bedroom, just seeing the excitement in their sons faces was enough to bring a smile to theirs.

'Please can we go outside and play?' Asked Owen

The parents looked at each other than back to their sons

'Of course but first we must all have some breakfast.' Replied their mum

The two boys jumped around with excitement, they could not wait to go outside and play in the snow.

Christmas at Stabdagger Castle.

By Andy Richards.

People all over the world like to keep the spirit of Christmas alive throughout the year in the hope of retaining the love and generosity it brings, yet usually the return to school and work destroys the illusion by reminding them of how expensive it all was rendering the festive spirit as dead as a coffin nail. Many people these days like to do what they can to avoid it and turn those winter chills into something a little more summerlike in fashion. But what about the other holidays of the year? Why not keep their spirit ticking over through the long months between their appointed time? People don't love each other just for Valentine's Day, and the magic of fertility isn't exclusively held during Easter after all. Somewhere in this dark and gloomy world there is a family whose blackened hearts are devoted to the holiday that celebrates the things that go bump in the night and keeps your nightmares recurring on a never-ending cycle of terror and torment. This is a family who belong to Halloween and have decided to celebrate the festive season the only way they know how. Everything was ready for them to try to understand the meaning of this thing they call Christmas except for one vital ingredient. They needed a feast composed of succulent flesh to gorge themselves as the humans do, but turkey was not on the menu. They needed something far more, shall we say, innocent?

The Christmas family vacation came to a standstill when the car broke down on a long winding road somewhere out in the middle of nowhere. It was the morning of Christmas Eve and they were already behind their intended schedule. The mother and father argued as the children kept themselves amused with their I-phones and game pads. The father's limited mechanical knowledge saw the afternoon turn to evening and the temperature plummet to a most unagreeable level. The lack of a mobile signal and absence of internet connection made a journey on foot inevitable, albeit most undesirable with frustrated protest from the youngsters. They locked the car containing the gifts and reluctantly left it behind, hoping that no one will find it until they returned.

The winds grew stronger as the snow grew thicker as the light grew darker over the land. The father led the way down the long winding path deeper into the woods with only a flashlight to guide the way. As tempers flared, and the pressure increased on the parents overstretched minds, a sight of potential salvation gave them hope on this most unpleasant of nights, for there in the near distance, through the branches of the ancient trees was a light from a window, shining like a guardian angel leading them to shelter, yet drawing them from the path that would have taken them to a nearby town.

Soon the family reached the edge of the forest and found a set of giant iron gates, beyond them was an ominous sight that made them huddle together in fear, the black silhouette of a castle against the bright snow filled sky with pointy towers and battlements that had stood the test of time, yet in spite of their collective desire to turn back the light shining bright in the cathedral like window offered the possibility of warmth and hospitality. The old iron gates took the efforts of the whole family to open, creaking and groaning like ghouls as they resisted against their efforts. The snow coated track that lead the way gave little to comfort the kids beneath long winding branched that looked more like the arms of the dead reaching over them.

Soon they stood by the imposing front doors lit by two burning torches fluttering in the wind. They all waited for the father to pluck up the nerve to reach for the iron ring and call for assistance. Running the risk of freezing to death the wife shoved him with her elbow and he reluctantly rang the bell. Heavy footsteps grew louder as they echoed through the house, the family huddled tightly as the doors creaked open revealing a tall, gaunt, creepy looking man who sent chills down their already near frozen spines. He looked down upon them with a sombre glare and a slight leer on his long stone like face. "Erm," said the father, "G... good evening. Erm, may we, I mean, do you have a phone we can use?"

The man's eyes rolled up as he groaned like a ghost. "No," he said in a slow, deep toned gravelly voice.

"Ok, erm,"

"We broke down," said the mother, "may we impose on the owner for a room for the night?"

"No."

"But, it's freezing out here, we have nowhere to stay," said the father. The children whimpered as they clung tightly to their mother. The tall creepy man was about to shut the door when a woman's voice was heard from within the darkness, "Greegore, don't be rude! Show our guests some courtesy."

He grumbled as he stepped back, "welcome to Stabdagger Castle," he said, and the family forced themselves to enter. They stepped over the threshold as the doors were closed behind them with squealing hinges and a loud crashing thud.

The house that greeted them was like something out of a gothic horror movie with an ornate staircase that split at the top. Illuminated only by candle light the place seemed to be decorated for Christmas, yet on closer inspection the decorations were more suited to Halloween, touched up with bits of glitter and tinsel. Standing by the split on the stairs was a tall beautiful woman dressed in a long flowing gown of black silk and webbing, with a smile on her pretty face that could send a chill through the hottest, driest desert.

"Greetings dear guests," she said, as a rumble of thunder ripped through the skies.

"Visitors!" said a man who seemed to appear from nowhere and made the family jump. He was dressed in a dinner suite complete with a cape and holding a decorative multi candle holder, illuminating his handsome yet unsettling face. "How delightful. I am Lord Stabdagger. Welcome to my humble abode."

"Thank you for accepting us at this late hour," said the mother.

"This is my butler Greegore, he's a gloomy old bugger but fear not, he'll take care of your needs adequately, and this ravishing creature is my beloved wife, Lady Stabdagger."

"It's, erm, really nice to meet you," said the father.

"Indeed," stated her Ladyship, slowly descending the stairs "it isn't often we have visitors, please tell me to what do we owe the honour?"

"Car trouble," said the wife.

"And today of all days. You poor things must be chilled to the bone. Please join us for a drink while Greegore gets your rooms ready."

"Erm, thank you very much," said the father.

"Mommy I want to leave!"

"Yes me too!"

"Hush now girls, let's not be rude to our guests," said the mother.

"Such delightful children," remarked her Ladyship, stood by her husband looking upon them with a strange look in their eyes, almost predatory. "Don't worry girls; we're going to take very good care of you all."

The weary travellers are lead to a guest room by the lumbering butler. A fire is lit and the couches are cosy. "What on Earth compelled you to travel these parts in this awful weather?" asked her Ladyship.

"It was going to be a family vacation," said the mother, "a luxury treat with my late father's inheritance."

"How tragic you must be devastated."

"Now the cars broken down we're not going to make it to the villa on time, now Christmas is ruined."

"Oh there, there, my dear you mustn't cry, all is not lost."

"Why not spend it with us?" said his Lordship.

"Oh we couldn't impose?"

"Nonsense," retorted her Ladyship, "you're here now and in just a few hours it'll be Christmas morning."

"We left all the gifts and luggage in the car," said the father.

"Fear not," said his Lordship, "I'll have them retrieved and ready for the morning."

"Tomorrow we're having a large feast. You will join us for dinner," proclaimed her Ladyship.

"We cannot thank you enough," said the father.

"The pleasure is all ours."

Greegore returned with a tray of hot chocolate drinks and they all supped heartily as the lord and lady looked on.

"How often do you have guests?" asked the mother. "Not half as often as we'd like," said his Lordship with a rather un-nerving grin.

"Yes, these days we never know when people are going to visit," said her Ladyship, "so we must seize the opportunity whenever we're able, and make a meal of every moment." The guests laughed politely as they drank. The children seemed ill at ease by the large oil paintings of long dead relatives glaring at them with lifeless eyes.

Soon the effects of the hot drinks were evident as the family yawned and struggled to stay awake. When the cups smashed on the floor the Lord and Lady danced with glee as the servants collected the dopey bodies.

"I promised you a banquet this year my love," he said. "Indeed you did you naughty boy."

They kissed and danced into the night as from the kitchens came the sound of chopping flesh and bone with a splatter of blood.

The blizzard raged as the fireplace roared as the winds howled past the castle battlements. Already the smell of roasting flesh filled the dining hall with its inviting aroma, teasing his Lord and Ladyship as they waited eagerly for the feast to be served. For it isn't just humans who celebrate this time of the year with a banquet fit for a king, monsters do it too, though arguably for much different reasons. "How much longer!" he said. "Patience dear, you can't rush perfection." He grumbled something under his breath before downing a whole glass of blood.

Her Ladyship observed the decorations to keep herself amused; human ribcages hanging from the ceiling covered with tinsel, maggots and flies, infant hands and shrunken heads dangling from the dead tree, implements of torture nailed to the mantelpiece over the fire, bloody handprints smearing the windows, the gifts fetched from the car ready to be opened, sitting beneath the tree among the gifts they had bought for each other. It reminded her of her childhood in the convent orphanage. Oh how she missed them and wondered what their troubled spirits were up to these days. "I wonder if we've got it right?" she pondered.

"What?"

"This Christmas thing. I mean, we've got all the decorations, the tree, the gifts and such, yet I still cannot understand what ordinary people find so appealing about it."

"Who cares! It's an excuse for good old piss up and a greedy spell of indulgence. That'll do me nicely."

"If this goes well, we might do this every year."

They were joined by their three children, psycho twin boys Tobias and Sebastian, and their deceptively beautiful daughter Carrion, dressed in an ornate dinner gown, and her fur freshly groomed, brushed and de-loused slowly descending the stairs. Her claw-like nails painted red, and her mane of hair curled into ringlets.

All three carried two gifts in their arms wrapped in black paper with blood red ribbons. "Merry Christmas mother and father," they all said in perfect unison as they handed over the gifts. "Why thank you children," purred her Ladyship, "We really are trying our best to understand this Christmas spirit thing."

"Shall we open our gifts now mother, or wait until after the feast?" asked Carrion, nearly drooling in anticipation.

"What do the humans normally do?" asked her Ladyship.

"Who cares?" said his Lordship growing decidedly impatient, fidgeting, muttering, with his empty belly bubbling and growling. She smiled at him sweetly. "You're so adorable when you're starving," she said, "reminds me of the night we first met." A twisted grin stretched across his face; then came the sound of the dinner gong that boomed through the house and caused anything that wasn't fixed down to move slightly. "Oh at long last!" he bellowed.

They placed the gifts down by the tree and glided hand in hand into the dining hall to be greeted by the whole servant staff and a spread fit for a house of undead kings. Greegore helped her Ladyship into her throne-like chair with her husband at the other side. The twins took to their seats as several staff tried to control the overexcited Carrion, running around barking and whimpering. Eventually they got her seated and then Greegore ordered the head servants to lift the silver domes from the platters to reveal a hot and steamy display of fresh roasted human flesh. His Lordship raised his glass of blood; her Ladyship raised hers in unison with their sons and daughter. "As the humans say," said his Lordship, "merry Christmas my dear."

"We really must do this more often. Cheers!"

Happy Halloween, I mean, Merry Christmas. (evil cackle)

Rod.

By Dave Bromley.

The light came on in the sleeping cocoon, and AR 194 began to stir. It was 6.7, the exact time when by decree children of the age of eight cycles had to be awake, exactly nine yonks after they fell asleep. As he stumbled into wakefulness, AR194 remembered he was not a happy boy. In four days, it would be RO Day, and he hated RO Day. It was so dull, with nothing to do. He could remember how bad it had been the previous year. He was sure that his parents also hated it just as much as he did; last year, all his Mother and Father did on RO Day was to shout and argue with each other.

AR194, or to give him his full name, AR/Euro/District 4/210985/194, lived with his parents in a pod circling Mother Ship 87 along with another hundred and twenty families. Although it was possible to move around the pod and visit your neighbours for most of the time, AR194 and his parents communicated with them using the iTalk device. It was so much easier than leaving their comfortable living and recreation quarters. AR 194's best friend was AR584, and they talked every day on their Wrist Devices or WD as everyone called them. Everyone wore one of these handy all-purpose communicators around their wrists.

As AR194 and his parents ate their morning food intake tablet, he asked his father, AR698,

"Why do we have RO Day?"

"That's a good question, son," his father replied. "I don't really know the answer, but why don't you Super Google the question, and I'm sure you will find out.

It struck AR194 that his father and mother did not know very much at all, but then they didn't have too, Super Google could quickly answer any question or query. Sometimes AR194 wished that he knew things, but now thanks to Super Google, there was no need for learning. Apparently, in long-lost times, children like him had gone to something called a school and learned things, but now no one had to learn anything because Super Google had all the answers. He had discovered about schools when browsing his Handheld Device, also known by everyone as HD because this was a society that loved acronyms.

Taking out his HD, AR194 said, "Why do we have RO Day?"

Instantly he got a response:

"Robots Off Day or RO Day for short is a hangover from ancient times when the people on this planet wandered freely around the globe. They did physical work and had a multitude of religious beliefs. One of those cult religions had a special day in which they celebrated the birth of their founder, a man called Jesus. His followers called this Christmas Day, but over time the religious significance became lost and it turned into a bacchanalian orgy,"

"What does that mean?" asked AR194.

"People would eat and drink too much, spend money they did not have and generally persuade themselves they were enjoying it. Today, they would not tolerate such conduct, enjoyment is very much a thing of the past. They would also gave each other gifts, especially to the children, also for some strange reason people sent pieces of coloured cardboard to each other."

"That sounds terrible," said AR194.

"I believe it was," confirmed the HD.

"What kind of gifts did people give each other?"

"Older people usually seemed to give each other things that the recipient neither wanted nor needed."

"And the children?"

"Toys."

"What are toys?" asked AR194.

"Things to play with. Fripperies, objects that serve no real purpose."

"That sounds like fun,"

"Do you think so?" asked the HD.

"Yes, but how did the children get these toys things?

"The children would write to someone called Santa Claus asking for the ones they would like."

"Who was this Santa person?" asked AR194.

"He was a fat man, dressed in a red cloak who would go out on a sleigh, pulled by six reindeer, with a sack full of presents for all the children on the eve of Christmas, I can show you a picture of him if you like."

"Yes, please," said AR194.

On the screen of his HD, a picture of a fat jovial old man with a flowing white beard appeared. He wore a red cloak with a hood and over his shoulder, he carried a full sack of toys.

"And all the children got some of these… err presents?"

"Apparently," said the HD.

"Surely, one sack would not be enough for all the children," said AR194, who had a logical mind.

"That is true, unfortunately in the annuls it does not explain how he did this, but our wise men have dismissed the story as a myth."

"But what if it wasn't?" said AR194, suddenly becoming interested.

"Some people, especially the children, believed in him. Apparently, according to legend, he came down the chimney with a sack full of presents."

"What's a chimney?"

"It was a channel from the house to allow smoke to escape. You must remember, the population lived an extremely primitive life back in the twentieth century."

"And to get these presents all the children had to do was write and ask for them?"

"So many children believed," said the HD.

"But what has all this got to do with RO Day?"

"The Grand Masters decided, in their wisdom, that the traditional Christmas Day should instead become the day of rest for all Robots, AI devices and Apps. A thank you for all the work they do on your behalf during the rest of the cycle. They called this Robot's Off Day."

"All robots and devises?" asked AR194.

"All except those on essential life maintaining duties. I shall also have a well-earned rest day."

"Thank you," said AR94 as he turned off the HD.

AR194 then began to think. This Christmas thing sounded like it had been fun, and he would have like to meet this Santa creature. It was all a load of rubbish and an ancient myth, but it sounded like it might have been fun.

Later that day, AR194 talked to his friend AR584 about this, through his WD.

"Sounds like a load of old rubbish to me," said his friend.

"Yes, but what if it isn't? Imagine waking up in the morning and finding loads of those present things at the end of your cot."

"You don't even know what a present is."

"That's true, but I think they sound like good things to have, and there is nothing else to get excited about on RO Day," said AR194.

"Well, I have decided I will stay in my cot all day. There is nothing else to do." With that, AR584 clicked off his WD, and the conversation was over.

AR194 pondered over what his friend had said; he respected his opinion, and to be honest, he almost agreed with him, but there was just a glimmer of doubt in his mind. He spent the next couple of days thinking about it before deciding to act. Taking out his HD, he said, "I want to write a letter."

"Very good," said the HED.

"Dear Santa Claus," HR194 began.

The dreaded RO Day finally arrived, but there was no wake-up call, which was the one good thing about the day. There was no gentle waking up music playing or health-inducing drink on the side table. AR194 also knew there would be no warmed clean clothing waiting for him to step into, and when he got dressed, he would have to put on the clothes left strewn over the floor the previous night. He delayed opening his eyes for as long as possible, but when he did, he got the shock of his young life.

Lying at the end of his cot were a pile of exciting looking packages wrapped in colourful paper. Quickly jumping out of his cot he started unwrapping the parcels, and inside he found many wondrous objects. AR194 did not know what most of them were, but that didn't matter; These were the first presents he had ever had, and he would enjoy them. The biggest parcel had a colourful card attached, and written on it was a message in old fashion writing, it said, 'Happy Christmas from Santa Claus'. Perhaps, thought AR194 this RO Day would not be so bad after all.

Christmas Chimes.

By Kate Brumby.

Christmas bells were ringing,

Their sound echoed all around,

Yet not one church member,

Within the building could be found.

No one appeared to be interested,

In attending the service being held,

Yet as the vicar looked out,

His heart was with peace filled.

He realised that church is people,

Not a building, so not so,

And just because none were there,

It was not a disaster, no.

It could be there was a gathering,

Somewhere else tonight,

It may be he just did not know,

As 'twas hidden from his sight.

It may that in meeting,

Friends were blessing one another,

So though he stood there alone,

It did not worry or bother.

For a few minutes he pondered,

And then at a distance he saw,

A man and woman appearing,

Followed by several more.

His heart was warmed fervent,

Seeing dozens of folk draw near,

And beyond four-legged beasts,

Were bringing up the rear.

Strangely warmed in his watching,

The vicar was astounded no less,

Knowing that this Christmas Eve,

So many'd be surely blessed.

Eventually all inside were settled,

And rousing carols were sung,

A joyous celebration of Christmas,

Followed with the bells being rung.

Throughout the year we'd do well,

To be reminded of this story wise,

And before jumping to conclusion,

Consider and think always twice.

No need to be disheartened, no,

God will always do His part,

In giving of Himself and others,

Making His church in our hearts.

The Present.

By Samantha Storey

A cold breeze swirls spreading the freezing sea fog deeper inland, swathing streets in eddies of a sparkling ice crystal laden mist. The odd combination of a bright moonlit night and a low creeping fog creates a mystical effect, ice crystals sparkling under the starry sky as fine as any newly faceted diamond. On a night like this you could almost imagine there was magic in the very air, weaving round your legs like the sinuous drifting fog, frosting everything it touches with glimmering possibilities.

Late night shopping happens every Thursday in the run up to Christmas, shops decked out with all the festive trimmings, baubles and tinsel shimmering in every jewel-like rainbow hue, fairy lights twinkling around heavily laden shelves and ever more creative window displays, enticing shoppers in with their wares. This particular

Thursday was bustling with bargain hunters all desperate to grab those final gifts on this last night of late shopping before Christmas, which falls nicely on a Saturday this year. Flustered parents drag over tired children along behind them from shop to shop with ever growing bulging bags of gifts and treats, bribing their reluctant shoppers with sweets to keep them compliant. Unorganised spouses, partners and parents struggling to squeeze all of their shopping into one frantic, rushed evening growing ever more frenzied with the desire to complete their purchases. The deadly trifecta of limited time left, being unorganised and struggling to find the perfect gift was starting to show in the strained, sweating faces of the shoppers dashing hurriedly from one shelf to the next. People streaming down crowded streets in pursuit of the perfect Christmas gift, the glistening sea fog tugging damply at chilled ankles and tired legs. Hurrying from aisle to aisle and shop to shop people set in a single-minded quest, a few stopping to chat to friends or neighbours passing them by, the festive spirit lost in the commercialised pursuit of their goals.

The run up to Christmas this year had been less than ideal with many high streets quiet and shops feeling the pinch with more people than ever before shopping online, luckily Greenthorpe had a whole raft of independent shops with unique, one of a kind and handmade gifts available, things rarely found online. Julie an easy going 19-year-old with the tall thin, gangly body of a girl not yet fully grown worked at the newly opened Rose and Reilly gift store on the seafront owned by two identical twin sisters of the same names. They were in their 50s and still did everything together, dressed the same, ate the same and even lived together, each with their own cat, grey tabbies from the same litter, brothers of course. It was as if there was a physical echo in the shop when both twins decided to work, on the rare days that they did work at all, so identical were they in their looks, mannerisms and speech. For months Julie had struggled to tell them apart and most customers still did, preferring just to lump them together under the singular title of twins rather than using their names and attempting to differentiate them. Julie was observant, so she learned to spot the three moles to the right cheek on Rose and two to the left cheek on Reilly, she had been brought up that way by her quiet, thoughtful father Julian. He had been a Twitcher, spending his weekends out looking for new birds to spot, teaching Julie patience and how to observe the very small differences needed to tell the often small brown birds apart. That was how he had died really, rushing off to do the thing he loved taking his devoted wife Susan, her beloved mum, with him.

Word had spread through the Twitcher's sites and chat rooms like wildfire, a rare once in a lifetime sighting of the Brown Booby in St Ives, Cornwall, yet another brown bird but the excitement and rarity of this one due to its unusual tropical habitat, not a bird ever seen in the UK before. Such a rare sighting was too much for Julian, running round the house in a frenzy of activity and excitement his floppy brown hair bouncing over his bespectacled, smiling face, he had his bags packed and the next day, Friday, booked off work all within half an hour of the first sighting. You had to move quickly when it came to spotting the rare birds or they quickly moved on and your chance was lost, his equipment including the new binoculars Julie had bought him the previous Christmas with hard earned cash from a summer job and a few changes of clothes was usually kept in a handy 'Go Bag' like some kind of gangster on the run. Julie thought it was great fun as a child, the family always dashing off somewhere new and exciting. Her mum Susan bringing along her latest knitting project to while away the hours and Julie a real daddy's girl insisting on having her own 'Go Bag' with binoculars, big heavy bird books with pictures to help verify a spotting and her own all important Twitcher's journal with the dates, times and locations added to the description of each bird identified. "Just like two peas in a pod" her mum would laugh, pointing out all the time how similar they both were with their mousy brown hair, freckled happy faces that needed at least a factor 50 in the sun in order not to turn a charming shade of lobster red. Julie used to secretly wish she looked just a little more like her mum, a true English beauty, tall and willowy with corn golden hair and watery forget-me-not blue eyes. She loved her dad fiercely and was proud to look just like him but the little self-criticising voice in her head sometimes laughingly told her that gangly nerd chic might look good on her dad but less so on a girl just trying to fit it with the kids at school. As she got older Julie was less keen going on weekend trips, preferring to stay at home to hang out with friends or watch tv like most 16-year-old teens, it definitely wasn't cool to hang out with parents all the time. Now Julie would give anything to have one more precious weekend with her quiet, nerdy parents and on her worst days sometimes wished she had gone with them that weekend.

The weekend her parents died Julie was going ice skating with her friends on the Friday night to celebrate finishing their final GCSE exams, it was like a disco on ice, lots of fast skating and most importantly boys, lots of boys and even one in particular that she really fancied, Billy Brentworth. Billy was the guy that most girls fancied, a few years older at 18 he could already drive and even get served legally at the off-licence, he was tall with bleach blond wavy hair. Julie wasn't sure if his curls where real or not and didn't really care, to her love-struck mind Billy had been a cross between a handsome surfer dude and her pop idol back in the day, Harry Styles. That puppy love had disappeared as quick as the morning mist when Julie was notified by the police what had happened to her parents, an out-of-control hire car driven by a group of young American tourists had hit her parents car head on driving too fast on the winding lanes of Cornwall. Her parents hadn't stood a chance, their little old Volkswagen Beetle although sturdy was driven off the road by the much bigger Land Rover and over a ravine dropping down twenty feet to a gully below. The perilous position of the crash had made it all the more difficult for rescue personnel to get her parents out of the car, her dad who had been driving died instantly and her mum died whilst being airlifted to hospital. All the tourists survived with scrapes and bruises, the driver receiving a caution and paltry fine for dangerous driving, their nationality and lack of video evidence or witnesses in such a rural area making it too difficult according to the police to pursue further charges.

Her parents had both been an only child and her grandparents all died when she was young, Julie didn't know if she had any extended family out in the world anywhere but nobody ever came forward to look after her. As she was only just 16 when her parents died Julie had to go into the care system and was housed in a large Children's home on the outskirts of Greenthorpe, her parents belongings and home were all sold and the few bits she was allowed to keep were put into storage, all assets were frozen until Julie came of age at 18. Her father had been a chartered accountant with the well to do local firm Perkins Myers, one step away from partner her dad liked to tell her with pride. Julian had been a financial wizard, making lots of savvy investments in stocks and shares over the years, building a nice portfolio that would have one day allowed him and Susan to retire abroad in style, travelling the world Twitching had been the ultimate dream.

Julie spent two years living in the hell that was the children's home, a big old Victorian building that used to be a private school, closed down in the 1980s crashing economy and sold to the local authority/ It was painted in shades of green and blue that were supposed to give it a calming feel but ultimately made it look quite institutional still. The 'Hell House' as she referred to it was always filled with arguments, chaos and endless changes in staff, routine visits from barely interested case workers were the worst, just a tick box exercise to make sure she had everything she needed, food, clothes and a roof over her head. Julie had wanted to scream at these monotonous meetings, "no I am not ok, no I haven't got everything I want, I need my parents Back!" She didn't though, why bother, nobody would listen, nothing would change. The two endless years a long drawn out imprisonment at the children's home, no family visits and friends were few and far between. You soon found out who your true friends were when your whole world collapsed. Some friends hadn't been able to cope with her constant grief and depression, unable to cheer her up and feeling uncomfortable around Julie not knowing what to say to her. Some friends really hadn't been friends at all and didn't even seem to give a backwards glance to her after the funeral when they headed off for a long summer of fun before starting college. Maggy was her only constant companion, a quiet plump sensitive girl with glasses and braces who had sat with Julie in form time at school and had made sure to text Julie every day if they didn't get a chance to meet up.

Julie had tried to continue on with her plans for college in the September, she had always been a top student who loved to learn new things, gaining all A's in her GCSEs. She started doing her A levels in Maths, English, Art, Biology and Chemistry, choosing to do five subjects rather than three, just picking subjects she enjoyed at school rather than with a clear career goal in mind. Just over halfway through the first year after lots of sick days, stress and depression Julie dropped Maths and Chemistry, sticking to the bare minimum three subjects, her favourites. The art lessons definitely helped to get her through the depression, many of her first-year canvasses were mainly angry shades black and red, deeply scored lines fiercely etched into surfaces, crackling with grief. Over time the anger left replaced by self-pity then a total numbness, the art changing to shades of grey and brown to match her spiralling mood. Julie kept to herself throughout college only making one real friend, Shelly who was a total force of nature. With her effervescent, unrelenting energy and unique stunning looks Shelly was universally loved by everyone who met her, which puzzled Julie some days as to why she would want to spend time with someone boring and mopey like her when all the fun popular crowd wanted to hang out with her. Shelly would just smile and dismiss her concerns as nonsense, maybe she didn't realise just how gorgeous she was with her translucent skin glowing like fine porcelain, delicate elfin features, huge luminous green eyes and long wavy dark red hair that seemed to glow with an inner fire. Yes Shelly was an absolute stunner but truly humble and kind with it, such a rare and amazing combination, she was always able to bring a smile to Julie's face and help her natural sunny disposition to try to reassert itself. By the end of college Julie had failed her Biology, scraped an E in English and a more respectable C in Art, plans for University had long been scrapped and she only had one goal at that time, to escape the children's home of hell!

The only thing Julie had wanted for her 18th birthday had been access to her inheritance and the freedom that came with it. She had long told her case worker her intentions to live independently in her own property as quickly as possible from the age of 18. Julie had been aged 18 years and 3 months when she bought her house for the full asking price in cash spending a good chunk of her inheritance and using a care-leavers grant to decorate and furnish her modest two up two down mid terrace property, getting the treasured parent's belongings back out of storage and finally back into use in her new home. It might be tiny but it was all hers, furnished with love and care, her dad's favourite ox blood leather armchair with a warm hand knitted grey, pink and cream throw made by her mum draped over one arm. Julie loved sitting in her dad's chair wrapped up in the throw her mum knitted, it was the closest she would ever get again to a big hug from either of them, many a night the throw had been drenched in her solitary tears. It was just over a year since she moved into her gorgeous little house, her bolt-hole from the world, a cocoon of safety wrapping around her like her mum's treasured throw. There were still some of her parent's things packed away in the loft, her dad's 'Go Bag' retrieved from the accident with all his precious

Twitching equipment, her mum's knitting basket with its built in pockets full of patterns and needles, the inside of the basket brimming full with as many balls of wool as Julie could squeeze in and the half finished cardigan her mum had been working on. Packed in storage for two years and then safely stowed in the loft, Julie hadn't felt strong enough to open them up yet and was unsure if she ever would.

When college had finished Julie allowed herself to wallow in self-pity for just another couple of weeks before deciding with the help of the irrepressible Shelly that she needed to get her life back on track and learn to have fun again. It was when out for lunch at the Disc one day with Shelly that she spotted the 'Staff Wanted' sign in the gift shop window. After a cheese and ham toastie and a big slice of a freshly made chocolate cake Shelly had finally talked her in to asking about the job, they popped next door and walked in on utter chaos. The twins had just had a stock big delivery and were struggling to carry all the boxes into the back of the store already busy and bustling with tourists. Offering to lend a hand and move all the boxes aided by Shelly whilst the sisters dealt with the customers really helped win them over when it had come to asking for a job. She had barely started to ask about the sign when they stopped her mid-sentence and asked her to start work the very next day. Julie loved her new job, no two days were the same, talking to customers, helping to solve any problems or give advice about a certain product and how effective or suitable it might be. The sisters, never very good at business or keen to keep regular hours had come to rely on Julie more and more in the six months since she started working there, training her up to work the till, stock taking, book keeping and even ordering new product lines from suppliers, Julie really had an eye for what sold well.

The shop had been inherited from their parents, once a cobbler's workshop belonging to their dad and his before that, it had ultimately passed to the twins with no male heir to carry on the cobbling business and neither Rose nor

Reilly every showing any interest or talent it was eventually shut down, all the tools and equipment sold off after their father's funeral. The shop occupied a prime position on the seafront in between the local quirky café The Disc with its unusual brews, homemade cakes and vintage decorations and the local library right next door. Along the same stretch of businesses was Petersons the bike shop whose family had owned the store for over 100 years, their hand stitched saddles were now world famous so perhaps the rise of internet shopping wasn't all bad. After Petersons was the local butchers Abernathy's, with all their hand made pies gleaming with golden egg washed crusts in the window and Christmas turkeys all hung up waiting for collection sightless eyes staring out at all who passed by. Greenthorpe was like the town that time forgot, it still retained a lot of family owned stores passed down through generations and all the charm of its Victorian heritage with stunning architecture heavy with mouldings and fancy wrought iron. The council and guild of local shop keepers only allowed independent shops on the main high street the giant chains were all kept out of town on the big retail parks. This divide seemed to work in Greenthorpe, the tourists and locals both loved the unique heritage of the high street and being able to buy fantastic quality hand-made products, there would always be a place for the mass produced stuff Julie was aware of that but it was certainly nice to have a thriving local community when so many high streets were struggling.

Julie liked to take her lunch breaks sat on the bench outside the library, more often than not eating a slice of her favourite lemon and blueberry Victoria sponge from The Disc, light, fluffy and airy the sponge was infused with sharp lemon and balanced with juicy blueberries bursting in your mouth and a perfect piping of not too sweet buttercream. Delicious! It was so relaxing just having half an hour to sit and watch the world go by, people scurrying past focussed on their tasks. Although having only worked at the shop for six months Julie was getting a feel for the rhythms of Seaview Street, the peaks in foot traffic at breakfast, lunch and just before the school run, tailing off again towards the end of the day. You tended to see quite a few regular faces out of season too, the locals who had been pushed aside by eager hoards of tourists over summer were the stalwarts of the winter season supporting their high street by continuing to buy local. The local library was always a hotbed of activity day and evening, used by a vast array of community groups from the Memory Lane Club talking about the good old days, sharing stories and swapping photos to the water painting club or amateur dramatics society who used one of the rooms to practice in.

One regular face was Edith from the Memory Lane Club, ever ready with a smile and desperate to pass the time of day chatting to whoever had a free ten minutes, Julie wasn't sure how old she was, somewhere between 60 and 80 perhaps, she had a smooth ageless face full of smiles and a chirpy twinkle in her eye. Most of the other Memory Lane

Club members seemed to be similar ages, all over 60 that was for sure, a few characters like Len with his shock of green hair and his studded leather jacket or blue rinse Mary with her glamorous head to toe vintage designer wear really stood out in the crowd, not your average pensioners by any stretch of the imagination. Len had once joined her on the bench in front of the library to sit and hand roll a few cigarettes whilst he waited for his bus home, they got chatting and Julie braved asking the question everyone wanted to know, "why the green hair?" Len had laughed and said, "that's easy, because I used to be a punk back in the day and still think Jonny Rotten is the greatest ever front man so why change my winning looks?" Len was hilarious after that day he would often stop by on her lunch break for a chat and to tell her the latest jokes he had heard, Len was obsessed with memes after his grandson had set him up a Facebook account. "Memes are definitely life." he would often chuckle to himself whilst bent over scrolling on his smart phone, Julie always loved to see Len, he was such an eccentric. Blue rinse Mary was a social butterfly always lunching with various friends or family members, she also went to nearly every club going at the library, just not the Slimming Club, "I certainly don't need that at my time of life." Mary would laugh patting her perfectly manicured fingers bejewelled in heavy diamond rings against her slim designer clad waist. Mary was absolutely tiny, like an exquisitely modelled doll, always perfectly dressed and well presented, hair coiffured and blue colouring touched up at her twice weekly appointments with Gerrard himself the best hairdresser in town with the most successful salon. Edith seemed like the odd one out in the little Memory Lane trio looking quite drab next to green-haired punk Len and designer clad blue rinse Mary, she was what Julie thought of as a traditional grandmother the sort you would see on all the Christmas family tv adverts sat in her rocking chair eating sweets in front of the fire or sat with her family all gathered round the big roast turkey dinner with all the trimmings. That reminded Julie it would be her second Christmas all alone this year, she hadn't had a big Christmas dinner since her parents died, the over cooked cheap food at the children's home had been awful and last year her first Christmas alone Julie spent the day in bed with a big tin of sweets and a bottle of water watching old films and trying not to cry thinking of all the times she had watched the very same films in happier times with her parents. This year Julie decided enough was enough she wasn't going to hide away and try to pretend Christmas didn't exist, she had already ordered all her favourite foods and was going to have a mini feast for one. Maggy and Shelly would be spending the day with their respective families but promised to pop round for a few drinks after tea, they really were good friends. Thinking of her own often lonely situation Julie wondered about Edith. By the way that Edith usually lingered in conversation at every given chance Julie suspected she might not have company at home or get visitors often. Edith always ended up at the bike shop after Memory Lane Club too, staring at the glossy red bike gleaming in the window. At this time of year it was usually children with their little running noses pressed against the windows and sticky fingers leaving prints all over the clean glass looking longingly at the new bikes and telling harassed looking parents, "this one mum, this is the one I want for Christmas."

Julie felt lucky she lived, worked and socialised all within a three-street radius which made it very economical not having to run a car, get taxis or use public transport, on nights like tonight that were really busy with late night shoppers getting a taxi would have been an impossible task. At the end of her shift turning the lights off Julie locked up the shop and set all the alarms, 10 o'clock and all is well she thought to herself. The swirling sea fog had grown ever thicker as the night has progressed and was no longer a magical veil of sparkling crystals, it had transformed into a thick, gloomy 'pea soup' of a fog. As she started to walk home once familiar surroundings suddenly morphed into lumpy distorted shapes that appeared to lurch out at her. Most of the shops had closed and turned their lights off, the final late-night shopping of the year finished, a few shop owners still lingered putting more stock out ready for the next day. As she neared the big shop, a figure appeared stood in front of the shop window, startled Julie jumped back a step as the figure spun round and advanced towards her. Peering closer through the fog she noticed it was just old Edith stood looking at the bike shop window. With a smile Julie walked up to her, "Edith what on earth are you doing out here at this time of night and in the cold and dark too, you will catch your death of cold." Edith smiled back snapping out of her private reverie, "It's ok Julie love, I only live round the corner, I often come out for an evening walk and to come and look in the bike shop window." Puzzled Julie asked her, "why are you always looking in the bike shop window Edith? I see you stopping to look after the Memory Lane Club too." With a sad little shake of her head Edith replied, "That right dear, I often look in Petersons, my dad was going to teach me to ride a bike, I had picked one from their shop window for my Christmas present, all glossy and red like that 'un over there. Unfortunately he died a few weeks before Christmas that year, I was only 8, my mum took ill with pneumonia not long after and never made it to Christmas either." Tears suddenly streaming from her eyes, the tide of emotion she had been holding back since her parents died finally breaking free with shuddering sobs wracking her body Julie clung to Edith searching for the solace of human warmth. "This will be my second Christmas all alone since my parents died." Julie sobbed. Startled, Edith rummaged through her big old leather handbag brimming with receipts, old bus tickets and the odd stray mint humbug searching and finally finding a packet of clean tissues. Handing one to Julie Edith smiled, "well what a pair we make love, both orphans and both home alone at Christmas, let me walk you home to make sure you get back safely, you seem a good bit shook up there and that's for sure." As they walked towards Julie's little home Edith carried on talking in a soothing tone stroking Julie's arm calming her with tales of her childhood and things that had changed in the town, which wasn't that much, really. By the time they reached Julie's house she was feeling calmer and lighter in mood than she had in a really long time. At her front door she turned to Edith and clutched her arm, beseechingly Julie asked, "would you like to spend Christmas day with me this year, I have ordered some nice snacks as we can have a little buffet and watch some films?" Surprised but feeling a warm glow inside Edith nodded her head readily agreeing to the invitation, "We can do better than a buffet though, love, how about I come early and cook a nice proper Christmas dinner for us? I haven't cooked for more than myself at Christmas in many years?" The kind offer to cook and the thought of her first real Christmas dinner in her own home brought fresh tears to Julie's eyes, her heart bursting with love for her new-found friend who despite their age difference shared so many experiences, Julie happily agreed.

Maybe tonight had been frosted with a magic fog of Christmas possibilities after all and to think most people remembered only the commercialisation of Christmas, too many gifts bought and barely appreciated, whilst tonight the memory of a special present drew two lonely people together for a heartfelt Merry Christmas.

Christmas in the UK.

By Ants Ambridge.

He warmed his hands on the fire. It'd already been a cold winter and now was only early December. The flat he lived in appeared barren. His living room contained a TV, the last remnants of his previous life, and a worn sofa, provided by a charity. On that sofa he lay curled up, screwing his nose in distaste at the faint tobacco smells that it still emitted, despite the amount of fabric freshener he'd previously used on it.

He pulled the blanket further around himself. He sensed the warmth in the room rising, which felt comforting. The TV showed an inane reality show in the background. He paid no attention to the relentless bellowing of the hateful protagonists. He contemplated changing the channel, but it would be the same story on them all, he guessed. His entertainment no longer entertained him. The thin, white curtains that remained in the flat when he moved in blew slightly from the draughts on multiple parts of the window. He hated those curtains; useless pieces of shit. They blocked no light in the summer and flapped constantly from the wind in winter.

Gaps through the curtains revealed the street outside, rows of houses seemingly trying to outdo each other with how gaudy a spectacle they made with their Christmas decorations. He quite simply couldn't afford to put up even a sprig of mistletoe this year, not that he would as he no longer held a reason to celebrate. There would be no turkey at Christmas for him this year, nor any family to share it with, not since he left his wife, leaving the kids with her. She'd protested, but he'd become a millstone around their necks dragging them down and he'd no ability to provide for them.

Three years previously, it'd been different. Christmas proved a happy time. He would revel in the overjoyed smiles on his children's faces as they anticipated the big day itself. Their excitement grew over the weeks leading up as they put up decorations, proud that ones they had made at school would be displayed prominently. Christmas TV specials began, so he and his wife would allow them to stay up later than usual to watch as a family, occasionally allowing them small amounts of eggnog or mulled wine. When the day arrived, the products of him and his wife saving all year piled under the tree, lovingly wrapped with bows and cards. He considered himself to be lucky to have such grateful children as they thanked their parents after opening each gift, even the clothes.

They would enjoy their dinner and spend the afternoon playing games with the children. He had always made a point of buying them both a board game each that they would endeavour to play as much as possible. He'd witnessed so many other parents who would simply get their children a games console and allow them to shut themselves away almost permanently. Whilst he and their mother bought their kids the same consoles, it seemed that because they attempted to spend family time together, their actions were reciprocated often. He missed the family, but understood it would destroy them to see him as he was now.

Then came the heart attack; in his thirties, an unexpected blow. The family, devastated and panicked, stay with him as he recovered in hospital. Pride forced him to adopt a forced bravado for them, despite the creeping terror of mortality. The doctors informed him he would need to undergo multiple operations over the course of his life. He didn't even remember the name they gave his condition anymore, the medication he needed to take made his mind fuzzy and caused sporadic memory loss. The main thing that concerned him; he'd been told working would no longer be an option.

His wife worked too, and for a while, they'd struggled with her low wage and his illness benefits. Then a further obstacle came when he was declared 'fit for work' and they stopped his illness benefits, despite the words of his doctors and consultants. He launched an appeal in vain, but they simply stated that their assessment was correct and that he needed to claim a benefit for people looking for work. Because of his wife's income, he wasn't entitled to the benefit they'd pushed him to claim, so he frantically tried to gain some other kinds of work that wouldn't put the physical strain on his weakened and failing heart. Every interview he attended, which were seldom, he helplessly watched the job slip away as they asked why the previous employment ended and he responded honestly. They would smile and suggest they were 'sorry to hear about your condition' and he wouldn't hear from them again. He understood perfectly, why would they want to employ someone likely to be off for several months after a bout of heart surgery?

He became withdrawn and worse, began snapping at his family. His wife shouldered the burden of providing for him and the children on a minimum wage. Every time he would verbally lash out at them, guilt and shame would wash over him and he began despising himself. His heart disease had become a cancer for the family. He couldn't take hurting them anymore, so one day when they visited her relatives, he packed a few personal items, including his gaming TV and simply left. He applied for a grotty little flat that no-one else wanted through the council and moved his meagre possessions in.

His wife rang daily for a few months, cajoling, pleading, berating. She tried to get him to come back, but the sight of his family suffering because of his own mounting bitterness pained him too much. Every time she called, he considered caving in and trying to work it out, but he perceived no future for himself. He repeatedly told her to forget about him and move on. Then she stopped calling, which devastated him even more. It was easier to be away with the daily contact, which proved the highlight of any given day, despite the hurt it caused the both of them. He still loved her dearly.

The TV crackled, and the screen went black. The sides of the TV began to drip, melting plastic dripping to the hardwood floor with a fizzle. As he predicted, the hardwood fireplace was a fire hazard and the flames from his overloading with parts from a broken chair had spread quickly. Parts of the floor where the plastic had melted on smouldered now. He turned and faced the back of the couch and curled up. He hoped his wife would know to sue the council for letting such a fire risk and by his passing, he'd provide adequately for the children, more than he would alive.

His back seared with the rising heat. He hoped the smoke inhalation took him before the flames.

A Winter's Tale.

By Mark Sandford.

North wind blows,

With it comes snow;

Chattering teeth and noses glow,

As winter displays it's glittering show.

Scarves and gloves,

Coats with hoods,

Wrapped up snugly to warm the blood!

Against the rains, I wish they would!

Beast from the East!

A Christmas feast,

Pigs in blankets at the least!

Mull the wine, cook the geese.

All this food, it'll make you obese!

Naked trees,

Gale force Seas,

What freezes up at zero degrees?

Brrr, it's cold and knocking knees,

Tramping down the crispy leaves!

Winter's won,

Watery sun,

The equinox has just begun,

Summer's done,

Dreams are gone,

Of lying on beaches having fun!

Star.

By Mark Sandford.

I saw the star for the first time tonight;

It came as a gift so bright in flight,

This star of mine.

And this night felt so right.

I saw the babe for the first time tonight

Wrapped in wool to keep him warm.

And I knew somehow that my life this night,

Was his reason to be born!

And the star shone so bright and so new;

For all the world, for me and for you.

Let it shine forever!

The Key.

By Victoria Hydes.

Jade yawned loudly as she raised her arms above her head and stretched out her entire body, well rested from her slumber. She glanced out of her bedroom window, surprised to see snow falling–the first white Christmas she could recall ever witnessing. Her mood instantly lifted, she slid out of bed, stepping into her pink fluffy slippers and coiling herself up in her favourite dressing gown, before shuffling through to the kitchen for a nice warming drink to start the day with.

It was her first Christmas living on her own and she decided, in that moment, that she welcomed the peace and quiet, the lack of decoration and fuss; just a small Christmas tree, a few fairy lights and her old childhood stocking hanging proudly from the fireplace, a yearly tradition she'd never escaped from, not even as she reached adulthood. She smiled to herself as she took a seat and switched on the TV, but her eye was drawn to the stocking. She could have sworn it was empty when she'd hung it, but now it sported an odd bulge, as though there was something inside. Curious, she wandered over and reached in, startled when she felt something hard and square graze against her palm. It was a tiny cardboard box, unwrapped, with a simple gift tag that said nothing but her name alone. No message, no sender, just her name.

She glanced down at the small pile of gifts in the corner of the room, mentally tallying all the possible senders to see if she could work out who might be missing. But no, everyone was accounted for. She sat back down, twirling it around in her hand while she sipped on her hot chocolate, her brow furrowed. Eventually, the temptation became too strong and she once again set down her mug, before carefully opening the box. Inside was a key. It looked old and slightly rusted, but bore an intricate pattern that gave it a sense of beauty and elegance, nonetheless.

Beneath it was a tiny scrap of folded paper. And that was it; nothing more.

She unfolded the paper and studied it closely, trying to make out what it might represent. It was a rather crude drawing, a far cry from a piece of fine art, but something about it looked familiar. She glanced from drawing to key and back again, realisation dawning upon her. The image was that of a gate, a very familiar gate, the old metal gate that closed off the overgrown passage by the now derelict school building. But why would someone anonymously gift her with a key to get in there? Everyone knew there was nothing left but intrusive vines and clusters of weeds.

She shook her head as she set it down, before finishing her hot chocolate, opening her other gifts and getting herself ready to visit her parents for Christmas dinner. As she grabbed her coat, she hesitated, eyeing up the box. She didn't want to tell anybody else about her find, but she also didn't want to let it out of her sight either. She hastily slipped it into her pocket, reached for her car keys, and slammed the door closed behind her.

The short drive through town to her parents' house seemed to last an age, and no amount of Slade or Wham! blasting over the radio could keep her mind off the small, hard possession by her hip. She glanced over at the old school building as she drove past, but resisted the urge to stop. She didn't want to be late, after all. Her mother would only be panicking, convinced she must have been kidnapped or murdered en route, or at least stressing about the turkey overcooking and getting dry.

"Darling, how are you?" her mother exclaimed as she answered the door. "It's so good to see you. Now come on in, don't be shy."

Jade hung up her coat and wandered through to the bustling living room, packed full with her friends and family, all except for one notable void, the empty space that two years previous had occupied her sister, Eleanor. When she hadn't returned from her travels last Christmas, the family were slightly surprised, upset that she couldn't even bother to see them once. But then they'd not even been able to get hold of her since, and she'd been absent from any kind of social media for a long time. Essentially untraceable. Jade often wondered what had happened to her. Her mother, bitter that she'd 'abandoned them' in the first place, had taken great offense and was convinced she'd just decided she didn't like them anymore, but Jade wasn't so naïve. She knew her sister and knew her well. She would have come home if she could, and even if she had made more exciting plans, she would have called to let them know. That could only mean something bad had happened.

Lost in thought, it took her a moment to recognise her uncle's voice, greeting her warmly. She loved her Uncle John. He was the only other person who seemed to see sense, who thought logically about things rather than living in an imagined fantasy all the time. Uncle John was often the one she'd go to if she had a problem, so much so that her own parents were actually blissfully unaware of half the stuff their daughter had been up to. From the heartaches to the crippling mistakes, it was their little secret.

Her fond memories were interrupted by the five little words that followed his hello.

"Did you get my gift?"

The way he said the words under hushed breath and with such a serious tone led her to assume he wasn't referring to the jumper she'd so gratefully received.

"Wait, it was from you? But what does it mean?"

"Just follow it, please, and before sundown. All will become clear soon enough."

She was desperate for more information but they were cut off by the announcement that dinner was served. She eyed him suspiciously, but he simply winked and smiled, before walking away from her. Now she was more confused than ever. If she'd thought the drive had dragged on too long, the meal seemed to last a lifetime. What would usually be a joyous occasion of drinking and laughing was this year a slow ticking time bomb, taking so long to go off that despite meaning her ultimate demise, she still prayed it would just hurry and claim her soul, already. All that mattered now was learning the truth. For all she knew, the gate could lead to something lovely, but she had a feeling it was instead some kind of elaborate scheme to test her, to trick her even. Uncle John was known for his practical jokes, after all. Even so, she still had to know for sure.

Jade excused herself early, much to her mother's disappointment, but she could make it up to her some other time. The temptation to enter through that gate had become too strong, and if she left now, she'd still have a few hours of light left.

She took a deep breath as she pulled up in front of the school building, shivering as a wailing gust of wind blew over the deserted street. She wrapped her coat tighter around her as she fumbled for the key, sticking it in the lock. As it clicked open, she turned back, taking a last long look at the white coated streets lined with twinkling lights and snow sculptures and wreaths. Everyone else was probably tucked up inside by the fire, drinking all their Christmas alcohol whilst recovering from their food comas, surrounded by brightly coloured gift wrap and stacks of new belongings. And then there was her, shivering and anxious and breaking into a dingy old ruin.

Even so, it was now or never. She turned back to the dark passage, carefully making her way through the thick foliage, stamping down thorns and pushing leaves out of her face, the brightness of the street shrinking, smaller and smaller, until there was silence, darkness, nothing to feed her senses but moist leaves and the crunching of fresh snow and rough earth beneath her boots.

She felt a rush of relief as the greenery began to subside and the low sunlight forced its way back through to her, and before she knew it she was standing in a small clearing of a patch of woodland, she didn't even recognise. She marvelled at the sight, the snow plump and undisturbed unlike the slushy mess that her street was becoming thanks to the traffic, the sun's rays glistening off the scattered patches of white that hugged the evergreen pines surrounding her. A couple of small birds flew overheard as she let out a small laugh. She was still no closer to finding out why she was here, but it was one of the most beautiful sights she'd ever seen, so secluded, unspoiled, like something from a fairytale. As she stepped forwards, she glanced around at every angle, taking it all in, before her eyes eventually rested on a small wooden sign sticking up from the roots of one of the trees. She crouched down and brushed off the snowflakes obscuring the wording, almost doubling back as she realised it was her name again, in exactly the same handwriting as had been on the gift tag.

She hastily dug around it a little to uncover another box, this one considerably larger than the one she'd received that morning. She took a deep breath before flipping open the lid and retrieving a single stuffed deer, almost identical to one she'd had as a child, before Eleanor had broken it in a fit of rage, that is. Jade had been absolutely heartbroken when she'd found it, its stuffing scattered across the room while one of its button eyes hung on by the thinnest of threads, but this one? This one was perfect. Her heart skipped as she admired it and she was so entranced that it took her a few moments to hear the light footsteps behind her.

"Hello, Jade."

Jade whipped around, poised to fight, but just as promptly dropped her stance as she gazed into a familiar set of eyes. She let out a small scream as she stumbled back, losing her footing and slamming down into the snow. She instinctively covered her face with her hands for a few moments before daring to take a second look, convinced she must be dreaming. But no, the figure was still standing right there.

"… El…?"

"Yeah, it's me… Look, I'm sure you have a lot of questions but there's not much time. I have to be going soon."

"But… what are you-? Where have you been? What?"

"I recently bumped into Uncle John by mistake, and he told me how much you missed me… I figured Mum would have just been bitter about my leaving, and I didn't want to spend the little time I have arguing with her, and so I got him to agree to keep our meeting a secret and assist me with concocting this little plan. Honestly Jade, you have no idea how incredible it is to see you again. I'm just sorry I made you worry so much."

"But why did you just vanish like that, without saying anything? I thought something terrible had happened…"

"I know, and that's precisely why I knew, no matter the risk, that I had to see you, to explain… You see the thing is, a lot has happened since I left and I'm not actually called Eleanor anymore… I-I'm living under a completely new identity now, you see. I didn't say anything sooner because I didn't want you all to worry yourselves with it, and the more people who know the truth, the greater the risk I'll be discovered, after all, which puts us all in danger. It was all going so well too until Uncle decided it would be a good idea to visit the very place I just so happen to be living now…"

"So you've been living a normal life this entire time?"

"Yes. I met a wonderful man on my adventures and we've recently moved in together. I have my cat and a steady job, and I'm still getting to travel a little too now and again. At the time it killed me to have to leave my old life behind, but honestly, despite everything I went through, becoming Lily is the best thing that ever happened to me."

Jade's mind was a blur as she tried to take it all in, errant thoughts and questions circling her brain as she attempted to retain her composure. Her only Christmas wish that year had been to see her sister again, and now here she was, clear as day. Dozens of looming questions finally answered, the guilt of encouraging her to go off alone on the trip she'd never come back from were beginning to subside. She was still concerned with what could have happened to require a change in identity, but she'd worry about that later. El was actually there, alive and well and genuinely happy. That in itself was nothing short of a miracle.

"Do you really have to go?" she pleaded as she found herself wrapped up in the familiar warmth of Eleanor's delicate arms.

"I'm afraid so, but I'm glad I did this. I think we both needed it… Merry Christmas Little Sis."

It was getting pretty late by the time Jade finally swung open her front door, damp from the melting snow seeping into her clothing and completely exhausted, yet at the same time all warm inside and wide awake. She poured herself some wine and lit the fire, curling up under a cosy blanket whilst holding her stuffed deer close, a comforting reminder that her sister was out there somewhere, living her best possible life, and not dead or enslaved or any of the other horrific things she'd at times imagined. She wished Eleanor hadn't had to leave so soon, and that she'd had more time to explain, but accepted that her fading back into obscurity was unfortunately the best thing for everyone. At least she could go to bed with sweet dreams that night, and would likely forever consider this the best Christmas ever.

Spaceman Came Travelling.

By Gemma Owen-Kendall.

It is always scary being on your own, seeing the days go by one by one, well it is for me, anyway. I can't believe it has been nearly six months since my heart got broken by someone I believed who loved me but instead chose my best friend over me. So I vowed for the time being I wouldn't love anyone on this planet in fear of it happening again. I guess you can still say I am only young and this fool was my first love, being only nineteen I still have a lot to live for, luckily, I managed to find a small studio and get by working every single hour under the sun. But living this way by being alone did not last much longer for me, I can remember the day when a bright light shone through my window.

It was coming up to Christmas and my full-time office job was forcing me to take annual leave so I had no choice but to take it as my department was shut over the festive period. I had decorated my studio with some tinsel, lights and a small Christmas tree with a star on top of it, in the hopes to feel a but better about myself I made a wish that the pain I was feeling would go away. Who knew that wishing on a star could come true.

I woke up to a snowy Christmas Eve morning, late morning to be precise but I think it was more lunch time as the night before I had watched a few chick flicks and down a bottle of pink gin. I lifted my head up off my pillow to the worse hangover I had ever encounters. Stumbling to the little kitchen area I downed a glass of water trying to come to my senses.

Later on that evening my hangover had eased off, so I managed to get out of my slump to go outside. The snow had slowed down and come to a stop by the time I got outside; I gazed up to the starry night sky and seeing how the stars were trying to break through the snow clouds. In the distance I heard a choir singing from a nearby Church 'Silent Night, Holy Night.' As I was listening to the lyrics and gazing upwards, a light flew across between the snowy clouds. 'Perhaps that was a shooting star.' I thought to myself but it seemed so near, so close. It was most likely my heavy hungover head playing tricks on me. I decided to head back home and call it an early one in bed.

That night I was woken up by a bright light shining through my window, I had no idea what time it was, it could not have possibly been the morning already. I ran over to the nearest window but the light was too bright for me. Then suddenly I was standing on the roof of the building I lived in, I didn't even know how I had gotten up there. I looked around to see a figure standing before me, he was the most beautiful guy I had ever seen. I had no idea where he appeared from but I could not help myself but stare at him. How embarrassing for me though as I was wearing my unicorn pyjamas, but he didn't seem to mind what I was wearing as he just looked into my eyes. His eyes were hazel coloured and his skin sparkled upon the light that was shining above us. It was like a flying saucer object just hovering over us.

He pulled me closer to him, his hair was chocolate brown, slightly spiker, for a moment there was no words that I could bring myself to say or ask him. There was something about him that was just out of this world. "Hello." His voice sounds as graceful as an angel, then reality started to hit me as I felt scared and started to shake. "Please don't be afraid of me, do not fear." It was like he was trying to make me calm down. "Who are you?" I finally managed to say something to him. "I am just like you, I have travelled from afar searching for you." This was beginning to sound crazy, but I liked it, I didn't care if it was just a dream or my hangover still taking over me but in this very moment my heartache had just vanished.

"You are just beautiful." Was all I could say back to him, he placed his lips so tenderly onto mine and I didn't want this moment to end. My head then got the better of me as it started to feel so heavy, I felt his hands catch my fall but still everything went black.

I woke up on Christmas day, late morning only this time I was feeling so alive and so fresh. It was like I had become a whole new person after my visit from a spaceman the night before. I had decided to get up and open my parents from parents that I had put under my little Christmas tree. There was one that I had not seen before wrapped in sparkly silver paper and tied with a silver bow. The label read:

I will return again.

Merry Christmas.

Love from your Spaceman.

Christmas Joy.

By Mark Sandford.

If we were there the night it took place,

What would our thoughts be back then?

Would we bring presents, and smile as we face,

The new-born King, in Bethlehem?

Would our songs be of joy?

Would our prayers plea for peace,

In our time and for all humankind?

Would we cheer for our boy,

With great vigour released,

By the news that we find, one cold night.

Fast forward in time, to the present day,

When we bring great cheer and elation.

When we sing loud and clear, in our Christian way,

For Christmas, and peace to all Nations.

Still Night.

By Eve Darwood.

She opens her eyes onto winter dullness. The window forms a box of grey behind the curtains, and she hears the puffing and chanting of the boiler, the chugging of water like a steam train through the pipes and radiators as the house creeks good morning. Her eiderdown nestles at her chin in folds and creases which match those on her neck, her cheeks, her forehead. The laughter and smiles, the forced fierce frowns for her children and grandchildren, the crumpled concerns of nights and days and years of worry and joy crimp her features into soft lines. She inhales, smiles, closes her eyes for a moment, breathing in the solitude.

She pads through in slippered feet to place the kettle, still half-filled from last night's cup of cocoa, onto the stove. The sky viewed from her kitchen window exudes the calm of an occasion. Even birds seem reverent of what the day will bring, their winged flights somehow hushed, like funeral prayers on cold oak pews. As steam rises, swirling, she shuts off the gas. Pours, stirs. Wrestles the plastic opener of a new milk carton. Before sitting to sip, she turns on the wireless to break the silence. A choir sings Hark the Herald Angels, and she hums the descant line while hugging the steaming cup.

She washes, dresses in her uniform of twinset, tights, the icy pearls she inherited from her sister.

They'll be hear soon, she thinks once she's cleared away her toast crumbs and marmalade. The sky belies the mid-morning hour, still murky, steely, cold, so she flicks on the switch to illuminate the fibre optic tree. The lights rotate within their prescribed colour cycle; red turns silver, fades to green, through blue, through turquoise, pink, warms to amber, burns to red. And again. She strokes the fading green velour of the armchair, right for lighter, left to darken. Watches three more cycles of the tree lights. Right, light. Left, dark. Draws circles with her craggy, now arthritic, fingers. Hears the music, now a pop rendition of what she recalls as Stille Nacht. Tuts and shakes her head as the young singer riffs her jazzy adaptation of the chorus. Sighs.

Holding his hand as they entered St Stephen's cathedral, their breath misting from gulps of the Vienna winter air. Scarves loosened, gloves twisted from their fingers, both of them mesmerised by the echoing voices, melded as one single soprano through the silent stones of the cathedral walls. Stille Nacht…

At her dresser, she rubs lotion into tired twigs of fingers, tries to soften skin she knows will soon be held in toddlers' hands, be ripping wrapping from a gift of scented candles, or more lotion, or a new silk scarf. Her fingertips press rouge into her sagging cheeks; she tries to emulate the flush of youth, of warmth, of blood that once would rise to her face at the sight of him. On this, her first Christmas morning without him, she tries to think back; when did she last blush at his touch? She counts in decades, not in years. Feels the sting of tears.

The car creeps into the space outside her window, its headlights sweeping a wave across her living room walls. Laughter tinkles into the air, three children bustle towards her front door, their chatter mingling with the radio's carols and cheers.

"Let granny get the door open before you all barge…" Her son's voice is lost in the excited chatter. He pulls her into his soft, firm arms, presses her face into his scarf, lands a kiss on her head.

"Hi Mum. Merry Christmas"

"Let me get the parcels. No, no peeping now, you cheeky rascals! There are some candy canes beneath the tree, just help yourselves. One each. Or two, it's Christmas! Let them treat themselves. Don't go telling mummy, mind."

With the parcel bags heaved into the boot of the car, she nestles into the seat beside her son. His hands on the controls–left hand sitting atop the gearstick, right hand cradling the wheel, just like his father used to do. His knuckles form the same rough crevasses. She steals a glance across at him, but he's distracted glancing in the rear-view mirror, checking on the children, who are sucking canes and singing carols she's not heard, and making guesses about what her parcels might contain. Hopes for yet more candy. "Granny always brings us chocolates, remember?" She smiles, pictures the scene later, the predictable pallor of over-indulgence witnessed every year the same.

The day retains its long-forged scaffolds of gift-unwrapping, long and noisy courses of smoked salmon, turkey, gentle encouragements towards vegetables on younger children's plates, the chinking of glasses–the crystal set of flutes that she and Henry had indulged in for them, somewhat extravagantly, last Christmas. When he was here. When he could grumble in department stores about the price of crystal flutes, and the price of train sets, and the price of scones and pots of tea when weary feet would interrupt their yearly all-day spree.

After dinner the children settle in front of a darkening sky outside the window. An animation snowman dances on the television screen, a sketch of a boy giggles, a half-familiar piano motif plays, her son pours her a sherry, places it on the circle of glass table beside her.

"Mum, there's one more gift you've not unwrapped", he tells her softly, handing her a neat parcel. Brown paper, decorated simply with gold hand-drawn treble-clefs, the way she's done it since the children grew too old for potato printing. A red ribbon, tied in a bow. She knows from the shape it's a music CD, for the player in her sitting room.

"It's from Dad. He wrapped it, before… well, in the summer, when he was still well enough"

Christmas in Vienna–the Vienna Boys Choir. Her eyes dance down the listings: Track 11, Stille Nacht…

She picks up her sherry glass, raises it towards the black-and-white wedding photograph propped on her son's mantelpiece. "Merry Christmas, Henry".

Pie-Eyed.

By Kate Brumby.

6 ounces (176g) raisins

4 ounces (110g) dried currants

4 ounces (110g) finely chopped candied mixed peel

6 ounces (175g) shredded suet

½ pound (225g) dark brown sugar

½ teaspoon nutmeg

2 teaspoons mixed spice

grated zest and juice of one lemon

grated zest and juice of one orange

cored and finely chopped cooking apple

Elsie looked at the list of ingredients–she had resolved to make her own mincemeat this year. December was the Women's Institute Christmas competition. Last year she had won with her decorated Yule log. Everyone in Gezegend Women's Institute who wanted to be involved was being asked to take along three different mince pies. Never being one to shirk, Elsie was going all out to rise to the challenge. Elsie wanted to win for the second year running.

Three hours well spent thought Elsie as she tightened the lid on a jar. Three hours and three good sized jars of mincemeat were ready to place in her larder. Each of the jars was slightly different–one with brandy, one with whisky, and one alcohol free.

There were two weeks before the Women's Institute Meeting–just long enough for Elsie's mincemeat to mature. In the meantime she would plan how to make her mince pies stand out from the rest.

Three different mince pies called for three different types of pastry–short crust, filo, and puff pastry. Three different mince pies called for three different shapes–a standard mini pie with a lid, a pouch, and one with the look of a turnover. With the combination of three different tastes, textures and looks Elsie felt sure she would do well.

The day of the Women's Institute Meeting arrived and feeling confident after almost daily practice making pastries with standard bought mincemeat Elsie felt ready to make her pies filled with her own homemade mincemeat. The whole afternoon was pleasantly spent and selecting from the batches of pies she had cooked Elsie placed three pies to take along to the Village Hall.

Elsie was pleased to see there were several plates of pies—of the twenty members eleven others had also decided to enter. As she looked along the line of plates Elsie was filled with pride—in her opinion hers looked fabulous, and she knew would taste just as good as they looked.

Rebecca arrived a few minutes after Elsie, wind-swept, she could have been described as a bit worse for wear. Approaching the table of pies she tentatively removed her competition entries from the box she was carrying.

Thirteenth entry, lucky for some, and perhaps lucky for her, Rebecca thought. Her three pies all looked very similar in size, shape and even colour. Nothing seemed to distinguish each one from the other two - not visually at least.

The meeting began promptly at 7.30 pm and as soon as Jerusalem had been sung, and the membership welcomed judging began. Marjorie and Joyce the Chair and Treasurer were followed by the group's Secretary, Beryl. Marks were being given for look, texture, and taste. Water at the ready to cleanse pallets Marjorie and Joyce made their way along the line of plates.

Elsie watched the two judges very carefully when they finally got to her entry. Marjorie smiled as she noted the three different shapes, and Joyce appeared to be impressed with the three different pastries–hers being the only plate amongst the thirteen with three completely different. A few of the other members had made different pies, yes, but with variations in shape and in top only. Some had iced the pie lids or added decorations or pastry lattice, but none had produced a plate like Elsie's.

As Marjorie and Joyce cut the pies and made their thoughts known to Beryl, Elsie looked on, and was delighted that when the two ladies tasted the pies they laughed–clearly tasting the alcohol within. Elsie felt both pleased and confident.

The final plate entered by Rebecca was then judged. Elsie was suddenly struck by the way both Marjorie and Joyce nudged one another, nodding and smiling. Glancing up at Rebecca, Elsie could see her face shining–she was a lovely young lady, very popular with the other members being someone who always liked to get involved with everything Women's Institute related in spite of working full time and having three children under the age of eight.

There were a few minutes whilst scores and comments were looked over. Marjorie called the room to order and congratulated everyone who had entered their pies on their efforts. All were silent as third place was awarded to Trudy, who had entered three short crust pastry pies–one with a standard lid, one with a lattice top made from almond paste, and one decorated with white royal icing.

The runner up and winner were about to be announced. Elsie looked expectantly, but was surprised to hear she was the one in second place, not first. Not first, not her, then who?, she wondered. Within seconds the answer came–Rebecca.

Surely not, Rebecca had three pies which looked perfect and unflawed yes, but the remit had been three different mince pies, not three the same. Unable to stop her thoughts from being voiced, Elsie blurted out her questions– "Why? What is so different about the pies that Rebecca has entered? Why has she won? Why have I been given second place?" Thankfully, she kept her other thought, of the judges being drunk and this having caused their error in judgement to herself.

Marjorie and Joyce were astounded at Elsie's outburst. Marjorie called the room to order once again and explained that Rebecca's three pies were perfect in taste, texture and appearance. They tasted different from one another though appearing to be the same.

Turning to look at Rebecca, Joyce tilted her head to one side and gently asked what it was that she had done to make each one taste different.

Rebecca smiled and said that she always enjoyed entering the competitions and that this had been the easiest so far. The entire membership gasped. Elsie was particularly taken aback as she thought back over her hours of preparation. What an astounding thing to have said, she thought. Rebecca continued telling all how she had realised that the simplest way to enter three different pies was to literally think outside the box. Specifically she had decided to think outside of three boxes by buying pies from three different supermarkets. One box from Tesco, one box from

Morrisons, and one box from Sainsbury's.

There was silence and then Elsie began to laugh, quickly followed by each and every other member of the Women's Institute. In the minutes that followed there were compliments aplenty as ladies realised how creative and clever Rebecca had been. Within her busy life she had taken the time to work out how she could participate, and she had.

Elsie was the first to congratulate Rebecca as she handed her the wooden spoon which was passed on by the previous year's Christmas competition winner. Elsie commented on Rebecca's resourceful nature. Here she thought was someone who epitomizers the Women's Institute, and someone to keep an eye on in future competitions.

Savouring.

By Kate Brumby.

"Cranberry sauce is all that's needed",

Chef announced to all stood there,

"With it the table will be complete;

Providing plentiful seasonal fare."

Here were roast parsnips aplenty,

Potatoes, carrots and broccoli too,

Not forgetting usual accompaniments;

Of brussel sprouts with nuts of cashew.

Boats of gravy in each of the corners;

Spouts pointing to the centre piece,

A huge turkey dressed with fruit,

Central to the Christmas day feast.

"Wait", said a voice from the back,

"There is something here amiss;

"I wonder Chef, if you would allow,

An addition to the meal of this?"

Holding her hands forward and up,

Upon them all looking sighed,

As she presented the Tsoureki bread,

Each their delight they couldn't hide.

"Perfect!" Chef exclaimed, "Perfect",

Indeed the finishing touch you have,

"I see the symbols wonderfully made,

Clearly designed and baked with love".

As all then stood back from the table,

Chef asked that all be quiet and still,

And after saying a thankful prayer,

He invited all to sit to eat their fill.

The colleagues and friends united,

Felt blessed by the food they shared,

The time spent this day together,

More than anything showed their care.

No one was eager to leave quickly,

In fact all were just happy to wait,

Each one savouring the moments,

Along with food upon their plates.

Chef made a final announcement,

In standing his message was clear,

"My friends, this day so wonderful,

Let's do similar now every year".

As if one voice all agreed fervently,

They would indeed this repeat,

Then raising a glass of wine,

Everyone got up on their feet.

A joint toast was made to Chef,

All praised him and the event,

And from that day to this,

Is how each Christmas is spent.

All I Want for Christmas.

By Victoria Hydes.

All I want for Christmas is some chocolate curls,

Or a jumper or some perfume or a necklace of pearls.

A precious pair of heels for a special night out,

And a bright red lipstick for the sexiest pout.

All I want for Christmas is a stack of books,

Or a frame filled with photos, complete with its hooks.

A movie to laugh at, and another to cry,

Or some mistletoe so it can end on a high.

It may seem a lot, but you get the gist,

I've been a good girl I promise, and thus I send you this list.

Black Lady.

By Mike Nelson.

I hated working in a pub. I hated men, wolf whistling at me or they try to grope me, even though I have been clear about my sexuality. Many blokes brag saying: "I can turn you straight." Or asking if I'm a "vegetarian? Because I like to lick lettuce." How mature.

Now I bet you're thinking, "if you hate your job, why don't you quit?" Well, you see the pay was good and there were some nice customers, and my grandparents, who I was living with, didn't live too far away, and I enjoyed walking home at night.

You see, I'm a nyctophiliac, I found the night relaxing and peaceful. Nothing seems to bother me, every night I would walk home to my grandparents. My route, would take me past me an old cemetery and a small path that was overgrown with nettles.

Nothing bad ever happened to me, despite getting stung by the odd nettle, and getting spooked by the odd deer jumping out of the darkness, nothing: Until Christmas Eve.

This pretty much started on the first of December, my grandparents, had continually asked me: "How I was getting home on Christmas Eve?" I just answered: "Walking" every time I would tell them that, a look of concern would come over their face's and with every passing day they looked more worried.

When Christmas eve, finally arrived both of my grandparents begged me not to go to work. But I had too, I need the money, and I had Christmas day and Boxing day off, so I didn't understand why they were so worried.

We had a heated discussion, then my grandfather said: "if she sees you." He said, his tone ominous. "just say you don't know, if you lie to her, she will haunt you ok?"

Confused, I nodded, however, my grandfather's tone sounded off and strange, so a little part of me took his word seriously. With that, I put on my hat, gloves and coat. It had snowed last night so at least the atmosphere felt like Christmas, and it was freezing cold.

Later that night.

It had been a long stressful day. The pub was packed, and I mean packed. Full of drunken locals, signing repetitive Christmas song. Wish it could be Christmas every day, was played so many times I lost count, also many drunken locals getting emotional listening to Mud's: Lone this Christmas. Then you had the crap from the previous X-factor winners.

To be honest though, the atmosphere was brilliant. However, the landlord, was asking time at 11:00. Weird, we always stayed open till midnight. "Why are we closing?" I asked the landlord. The landlord turned, "Don't ask questions!" he said. "make sure you're home before midnight."

I rolled my eyes and shook my head. Even the landlord was acting strange, but this did tickle my curiosity, so I took my time getting the barware cleaned; dragging out the time basically.

11:45: the landlord, pretty much had to boot me out of the pub. "GET HOME NOW." He ordered. "and a merry Christmas." I wished him the same and did as I was told and began to walk home in the bright cold moony night.

It was so beautiful, the moonlight shining on the snow had given the bright cold white light. It was cold yet soothing. I stood on the path and soaked in the wintery atmosphere. I was in my own little world until my phone rang.

I went to answer it and check the time; 11:58 and it was my grandad, "hello?" I asked. "TWO MINUTES GIRL GET HOME NOW." He then put the phone down. I let off a sign and continued walking, alone with only the sound of crunching snow to keep me company.

CHURCH ROAD:

I sped up my pace and was about to walk down Church Road, and this is where everything started to get weird. I checked my phone; it was dead. Strange, it was on 95%. Shrugging my shoulders I pulled out my battery bank, however, that was dead.

I stood in the snow puzzled. Suddenly I felt like something was watching me from behind, I turned around: nothing. But I felt compelled to keep walking and as I did, things got stranger. "where are all the lights?" I thought. The entire road was engulfed in the dark moonlight. "did everyone become a Scrooge and decided to ban Christmas?"

For the past few weeks, the road had lit up by a warming Christmas glow, but tonight it was eerie, spooky and dark. I shudder of fear had consumed me, what was wrong with me? I'm usually not like this. I've never been scared of the dark, nothing was adding up yet. I continued walking.

Every step I made the more scared I got. The silence only being broken by my footsteps. I quickly sped up. But the deeper I got down the road, the more paranoid I felt. To calm my nerves, I started to hum Christmas songs and thinking about tomorrow's Christmas dinner, but an ear piercing scream had put a hole in my plot.

I was paralyzed. I couldn't move. I wanted to go home. Then I started to hear footsteps, then a dragging of chains, then a weep and then a wail. It was getting closer and closer and closer until....

Standing only a few yards from me was a woman. My mouth dropped over the sight of her. Her hair, eyes, lips were black. Her toes and fingers were rotten with frostbite. Her skin was grey and lifeless. But her entire body had been mauled and broke, she was covered in stars and her left arm was broken, and her right foot pointed the wrong way.

Her neck, wrists and ankles were bounded by chains. Who was she? I froze in fear at the sight. I had to move, so I tried to walk around her but in the ultimate horror cliché, I stood on a stick. The loud "SNAP." Had got her attention.

She then started to walk towards me. I wanted to run but I couldn't my legs just wouldn't function. As she got a few feet from me, a horrid stench started to suffocate my nostrils I was choking on the smell, I couldn't breathe, I wanted to throw up but I couldn't.

She was right in my face. I nervously looked her in her maggot-infested eyes. She then untied the cloth around her head, causing her jaw to drop; maggot, worms and dirt pouring out. "what do you want?" I asked. "please don't hurt me."

She then lent in. "daughter?" she whispered. "where's my daughter?" I didn't know what to say. Wait, was this what my grandad was on about? I couldn't remember what he said." Erm… she's over there." I responded, my arm shaking while I pointed.

She then slowly backed off and started to walk in the opposite direction. A few seconds passed and she'd vanished into the darkness. Not wanting to wait around, I quickly continued down the path hoping to gain some grown and praying I didn't slip in the snow, but that's was not to be.

As soon as I turn the corner and got passed the cemetery's gates. She screamed like a banshee. "LIAR! LIAR!" I turned around, and she was charging straight toward me, her body contorted; running on her hands and feet, her grotesque head and turned a full 180.

"NO, LEAVE ME ALONE.! I screamed. I closed my eyes. She was going to kill me. It felt cold, really cold, and that's all I remembered, I must've passed out.

When I opened my eyes again, I was in my bed, with a bandage wrapped around my head. Was it a dream? I slowly got out of my bed and checked the mirror. My fear had come back, scarred on my stomach in big black writing was the word "LIAR!"

I let out a huge scream and ran downstairs. Both my grandparents were sat in the kitchen drinking coffee. "grandad" I cried while I showed him the mark. He shook his head. "I did warn you, my girl." He responded. "who was she?" I asked.

My grandparents look at each other, then my nanna walked out of the room, her eyes had started to tear up. "we don't know her name." grandad explained. "however I do know her story but I warn you, my girl, it is quite upsetting." Not the best way to start Christmas day. I wanted to open my presents, but my curiosity had got the best of me again. So I nodded at my grandad, he then took a huge breath and proceed to talk.

"Years ago a woodsman lived with his wife and daughter." Grandad explained. "however, one day he was forced to fight in the War of the Roses." He then took a huge gulp of his coffee. "that poor woman." He said "for months she'd walked to the edge of the woods, hoping to see her husband had returned." Shaking his head. "Christmas eve that year, soldiers from the opposition had invaded the woods, found her…" grandad then paused.

Stood up, looked out the window and stared straight at the cemetery. "they found her brutally spent the day raping and torturing her." My grandad started to cry. "then on the stroke of midnight, she was bounded and her daughter was murdered in front of her, then she was killed."

I broke down, that poor woman. "it is said, every Christmas Eve on the stroke of midnight she walks around the woods, village and even the nearby pitches. In a feeble attempt to find her daughter." He then looked at me straight in the eyes. "you saw her?" he asked "and she asked you the question?" I nodded, "I pointed because I was scared." I confessed. My grandad's mouth dropped and a bead of sweat dropped down his head.

I shook in fear. "What will happen now?" I asked. "she will haunt you." Grandad responded loudly. I didn't want to ask my second question, but I had too. "what will she do to me?" grandad's head turned sharply: "I don't know." Black lady.

12 Sins of Christmas.

By Rebekah Richards.

This was it; the moment he had been training his whole life for. He was finally following in his father's footsteps; finally going to be able to wear the big coat. He was going to be Santa Claus. Harry had dreamed of this moment ever since his father had done it. His father had helped him to train, teaching him all the tricks of the trade. They made a game out of it, training together while his father was on the waiting list for his turn at the big red coat. His father had begun preparing him from the age of 5; it was a family business. Every male on his father's side took a turn at being Santa Claus, although they only ever did the job for 1 year. Hank's father was determined that he would do the job for longer; that's what they all wanted. Unfortunately, his father died in a car accident while drunk, around Halloween and so he, like all the ones before him, only did the job for a year. His father was not strong enough for the role. After completing his year's employment, he had turned to alcohol to help him cope, and that was ultimately his downfall. Hank was different; he would be the best Santa Claus that the world had ever seen.

Hank supposed in some respect he wanted to prove it to his father as well as himself that he could do the job. He had been preparing hard for the tougher aspects of the role. Hank couldn't wait until the day he receives his list. He was ready. In fact he was born ready; this was his destiny. What happened to last year's Santa Claus? He didn't know and frankly he didn't care. He had been waiting 4 years for his turn. Rumour had it that last year's Santa was holidaying somewhere, sunning it up on some tropical beach. What was the point of taking the role if you only intended on serving one year?

A knock on the door broke him out of his daydream. His delivery had arrived at last; the big red suit. Hank tried it on for size, admiring his reflection in the mirror. It was a perfect fit, of course. These suits came custom-made. His employer must spend a fortune on getting a new suit tailored every year. Well he would save them money for sure. There was no way he was quitting at the end of the year and to hell with the easy way out of committing suicide. His stomach was made for this. He carefully folded his suit and put it neatly in his wardrobe. Time for wearing that will come later. He sat cleaning the tools he will need to pass the time while watching the latest slasher film to be uploaded to Netflix. It was just the type he liked to watch to get him in a good mood. Blood, guts and gore. Lovely. He was getting excited now. First the suit, next the list. Let the fun times begin.

Two weeks had passed since he first received his suit; he had taken it out of his wardrobe at least once a day since then to admire it. Today was the day he would be receiving the first name from his list. This was it, he had one week to prepare for his first assignment; after that his list would be arriving daily; time to put all that training into practice.

He could not contain his excitement. The anticipation was almost overwhelming; it reminded him of his younger years when his father had taken him hunting and the joy he felt after he had made his first kill. Hank was getting restless; nothing occupied him for more than 5 minutes before he once again would get up to peer out of the window looking for the elusive post-person to arrive. He would use this first week wisely to plan his approach to the role as once the first assignment was over there would be no time for planning. He desperately wanted to make an impact; to impress his employer. It was crucial to him that he could continue in the job longer than anyone else. He has started to make it his lifetime ambition. He began to pace backwards and forwards across his living room, the already threadbare carpet unable to take it anymore began to tear under the extra strain of his pacing. Never mind, he would soon be able to afford to replace it once he got paid. Unable to hold down a job in the recent years due to his unwillingness to accept anything but his dream job, the house had fallen into disrepair.

He tried to distract himself; to stop focussing on receiving his first assignment but he was just growing more and more frustrated. At long last the postman started heading up the driveway; a bundle of envelopes in his hand. The tinkle of the letterbox followed by a thud, gave him so much excitement he felt like a child at Christmas. How ironic, he thought to himself idly as he retrieved the mail. He filtered through the usual drivel; bills, postcard from his latest fling and junk mail. It was then he saw it; the envelope he really wanted; A4 size, gold envelope with black cursive handwriting and double sealed with extra pieces of tape to avoid anyone else opening it. He took out his letter opener and carefully sliced through the tape; his heart threatened to beat out of his chest. His hand shook as he took out the documents contained within. Humming his favourite Christmas tune to steady himself, he glanced at the picture of his first assignment. He chuckled to himself at the new lyrics he had created. His assignment was Ivan Meadows; last known place of residence, Suffolk. He studied the photograph more closely. This would be easy. "Merry Christmas Ivan. Here's to a better new year". He toasted to the picture. Time to get to work.

Ivan, it so happened, was a burglar, a very violent burglar, and so it was that he was the first name to be added to the naughty list. It is of no surprise therefore, that he needs to be punished. Only good people were rewarded with presents and such like, but delivering presents wasn't something Santa did. Not these days. This was a common misconception held by the masses who had read too many of the feel-good fairy tales to their children in an attempt to teach them to behave. Yet, none of them ever questioned that they had to do the Christmas shopping, too happy to believe, once grown up, that Santa must be nothing more than some fictional character. Naturally, as with all fictional characters, they often have some basis in fact. The fact was that Santa existed to punish the naughty and so there was no need to reward the good as the fear of the consequences of being naughty would make everyone good. Or at least that was the theory. Clearly the fact that there was still a need for a Santa Claus proved that it wasn't too big of a deterrent. He would change that; soon everyone would be singing his new signature song and word would get out.

"Well Ivan", he said to himself, "your days are numbered.

The next week passed by in a flash, planning moves and countermoves; every little detail of the punishment he was going to deliver was now so ingrained into his mind it was almost as if he was watching a film reel of the deed already done. He could almost picture the look on Ivan's face already when the realisation that he has been caught suddenly dawns on his face. He couldn't wait to see that expression up close and personal. Tomorrow was the day. All of his tools were prepared; his suit lay neatly on a chair by his bed ready to slip on in the morning.

Waking up early the next morning, he took a shower, cherishing the feel of the warm water running down his torso. He wanted to look his best for his first day. He spent what felt like an age in the shower, distracted in his own thoughts. He played the impending scene over in his head a number of times before he realised he was still in the shower and that if he didn't get a move on he would soon miss the deadline. He dried quickly and dressed at long last in the signature red suit. Glancing one last time in the mirror, he made his way out of the door, picking up his tool bag as he went.

"Ivan, I hope you're ready. I'm coming for you". He muttered to himself as he jumped into his car and set it in reverse to back out of his drive. Turning up the radio, he began singing along to the usual Christmas songs, changing some words here and there to his own version. If he was left in charge of writing Christmas songs about Santa Claus, the whole world would know the true meaning behind the 12 days of Christmas. True. The message was very much the same that in order to be rewarded you must be good, but no one was brave enough to mention the true consequences of being bad. Not him; he would shout it from the rooftops. He followed the ever-winding roads that would eventually lead him to Ivan.

Hank pulled up outside Ivan's house. There was a light on shining from one of the upstairs windows; shadows on curtains told him that someone was home. Now was the time to put his plan into action. He walked up casually to the front door; it would be better for him to gain easy access. Ivan answered on the 3rd knock of the door. Hank forced his way past a confused looking Ivan and walked into his living room. This one would be quick and easy Hank thought idly to himself; after all he had been deemed the tamest of the assignments by simply being the first on the list. Each target was supposed to be more violent and committed nastier crimes as the 12 days progressed. Still, Hank wanted to leave a clear message. This was why Ivan would be dying by his own weapon of choice. Ivan often brandished a crowbar to make his victims more persuasive of parting with their treasures. It was only fitting therefore, that a crowbar was what killed him.

Ivan did not disappoint; the expression Hank was expecting was even better when viewed in close proximity rather than his own imagination. Confusion, shock, horror and fear all rolled into one crossed Ivan's face as Hank swung the crowbar repeatedly at him, until all that was left to express was sorrow, with maybe a hint of remorse. Ivan's body fell to the ground, never to terrorise anyone again. Assignment one was complete.

Hank took the long winding roads back home, unlocked his front door and glanced down at his doormat. There, in a gold envelope, sat assignment number two. He picked up the envelope and place on his side table to look at after he finished getting himself cleaned up. Taking a brisk shower this time, eager to see his next task, he dried quickly and ran downstairs to retrieve the envelope. Carefully he slid the letter opener under the flap not wanting to tear any crucial information contained within. He took out the contents and glanced at his next assignment.

His second assignment was just as easy as the first; probably easier in fact; a dodgy drug dealer. A simple overdose of her own stock will be sufficient to put her dealing days to an end. Hank had decided on his drive home the previous day that he need to tone it down a little. He had gotten too carried away on his first assignment; shown his hand too soon. He needed to save that level of violence for the worst of the worst. Bashing Ivan's head in was one thing, but writing 'Santa Claus is coming to town' on the walls in Ivan's blood was over the top. He would get his recognition soon enough. He just had to be patient.

The day went smoothly just like he had planned. Cynthia let him in almost instantly after he mentioned wanting to score. She was a rather attractive woman; shame she was dirty and rotten. A few drinks and some flirting later and she was lying dead on the living room floor after being given the fatal dose. He didn't think she would agree, at first, to shooting up together but once she did all he had to do was to ensure he prepared the needle and insist on ladies first. The rest as they say was history. Hank took a photograph of her body where it lay on the floor; a hunter wasn't a hunter without his trophies. He returned home feeling deflated; there was something about an overdose that left such an anti-climax. His intrigue soon picked up, however, when he spied a familiar glint of gold on his doormat.

Unfortunately for Hank, the next two assignments were very much the same sort of theme. Drug dealers; they were too easy to get rid of and Hank was soon getting bored. The only relief from insanity came from his little attempt at humour when on approaching the third drug dealer; he decided to frame it to look like this one had been killed by his previous one. That would keep the police confused for a while; he chucked to himself as he drove away, praying that when he got home, it would be to a more interesting and challenging opponent for tomorrow's advent. He longed for something that he could use to express his pent-up frustrations. He wanted variety; to put his skills on show; to prove why he was the best man for the job. He was longing for the thrill of the hunt.

After once again taking his routine shower upon his arrival home, Hank settled down in his chair by the fireplace and opened the latest envelope. He had gotten his wish; an armed robber who stole at knife point. Well that made choosing a weapon easy; Hank was nothing but consistent, if a criminal had a weapon of choice or something that could be turned into one; you could bet your bottom dollar Hank would utilize it to bring about their end. It was only fitting therefore, that his latest assignment died at knife point. All Hank had to do was choose the point of entry.

The next day passed by quite quickly; a short drive took him to his destination and landed him at the home of assignment 5. Hank quickly dispatched the man, not wanting to mess about with the theatrics for this one. He would save his best work for those more deserving. The relief at administering a more violent end was exquisite. He felt like a hunter once more. Taking his picture with the posed body, he left making a stop at a local takeaway on the way home. He deserved a treat now he was almost halfway through the list, he reasoned. Cleaning himself up, Hank settled down with his chicken chow-mein, sweet and sour pork balls and duck spring rolls. He had taken care of this assignment so quickly, there was no letter waiting for his arrival home. After finishing his takeaway, Hank cleared away his pots and tidied his kitchen. The familiar tinkle of his letterbox sent electricity coursing through his veins. This was it; his next assignment. He picked up the envelope gleefully and wasted no time in opening it.

The following morning Hank got up and dressed early; it wasn't a long drive to the next location, but he wanted to drag this one out for as long as possible. On arrival to the location, Hank glanced around his surroundings. The location was perfect. No nearby houses, hardly any traffic, no one to hear the screams; simply perfect. Hank didn't waste any time trying to gain a peaceful entry, instead he just broke down the door and used the element of surprise to subdue his latest prey. He secured the door to ensure his next assignment, the rapist, couldn't escape and started his torture. First, he roughed the guy up a little; he had looked too clean for such a violent thug. Once Hank was satisfied the guy looked rough enough, he took out his set of surgical knives from his tool bag. Inspecting each one carefully he finally made his selection, choosing to use the bluntest one of the lot. He didn't want the cut to go too smoothly, it was much more painful with a blunted blade. He tore off the man's trousers and took hold of his member. Slowly and with the utmost precision he started hacking away at the man's penis cutting off inch by painful inch until nothing remained but an open, gushing wound where his penis would have been. He left the man sat tied to the chair for a good long while to enjoy the screams.

He demanded the man to tell him why he would have done that and why he was there. Hank wanted the man to acknowledge the things he had done. When eventually the rapist did give in and give his explanation, only then did Hank strangle him, like he had his victims, and put him out of his misery. Hank took his trophy photo and this time his recording of the screams and left; all too eager to see what tomorrow would bring.

Tomorrow, as it so happened, brought Hank face to face with Albert; the neighbourhood arsonist. Hank managed to gain the guy's trust long enough to get Albert into his car; he wanted to choose his own scene for this one. He drove Albert to an old abandoned warehouse building where he then doused him in petrol and set him alight. It was only fitting that he died this way when he had such a love of fire. If anything, the way it was set up looked like it could have been another arson attempt gone wrong. Taking time to roast a few marshmallows before the flames became too aggressive, Hank took time to reflect on the week he had so far. True it was a little boring at the beginning but now things were truly looking up. He felt almost sadness at the fact it would soon be coming to an end.

On arriving back home, he carefully stepped over the mail on his doormat and instantly saw not one but three envelopes. Curious as to why three assignments had arrived in one day he scooped up the mail quickly and began to open them. It soon became clear why. These three people were part of the same gang of kidnappers. They were still intended to be spread out over 3 days but the information had come together in order for him to link in the deaths. He would have fun with these. Deciding instantly that the ringleader would be left to last Hank set his plan in motion.

After killing the first gang member Hank drove past the house of the ringleader in the middle of the night and posted photos of the first member at various stages of torture through the letterbox. He wanted the ringleader to know that he was coming for him and that there was nowhere to hide. He also installed a tracker to the ringleader's car so that should he try to run he would be easy to track down. The following night after killing the second member, Hank once again returned to where the ringleader was hiding. This time he posted body parts from the second gang member along with photos of torture. Finally on the third night it was the ringleader's turn. The fear etched into his face as Hank broke his way into his hiding place was enough to get Hank's adrenaline going. He tortured the ringleader long into the night before eventually slitting his throat, when the screams became too tiresome. There was only so much self-pity his ears could take.

At long last it had come down to the penultimate assignment. This one was a murderer, of no fewer than 5 victims. He seemed to have a pretty set routine as to how he killed his victims. Hank studied this carefully. He wanted to be sure that he got every detail correct, as this one would be dying by his own method. He took every detail into account; how to get the guy in his clutches in the first place, location, how the final fatal wound was inflicted, the type of blade used; everything. The whole ordeal, once planned lasted around 2 hours from securing the guy to posing the body and taking the final picture. Tonight the last assignment would arrive and this time tomorrow would mark his yearlong holiday ready to strike next Christmas.

Hank opened the envelope of his last assignment; the picture within showed a man in a red suit. He would know one of those suits anywhere having owned one for the past month himself. He knew before even opening the documents detailing the crimes that this must be the Santa Claus from last year; this was why they only lasted a year. As much as he knew it as true, Hank still went on to read why this man had made the list. He didn't want to believe he had been set up, but upon reading the rest of the way through the file it was there in black and white. This man had made the list due to killing 12 criminals last year. No doubt this would be his fate this time next year. He felt tricked, cheated, angry at being set up. He knew just how he would handle his last assignment.

Hank sat up late that night preparing his approach. The careful planning of the weeks leading up to this now no longer needed; he had a new plan for this one. He chuckled to himself as he added 3 more verses to the song he had been working on that he intended to send to the newspapers. This was how he had intended on getting his recognition; to get the word out about what his job entailed. He had new intentions for it now. He changed the address on the envelope to that of his employers and set out to find last year's Santa. He would need help and lots of it.

The next day in some secret government run building, the tape made its way through the internal sorting office and landed on the desk of one of the employers. Doing as instructed she took out the tape, inserted it into the tape

recorder and pressed play. This is what
she heard.

You better watch out,

Don't commit a crime,

Cos there is no doubt,

You'll pay with your life,

Santa Claus is coming to town.

He's making a list,

Checking it twice,

You'd better hope that,

He thinks you are nice,

Santa Claus is coming to town.

He'll kill you when you're sleeping,

He'll maim when you're awake,

He'll hunt you down if you're not good,

So be good for goodness' sake.

You'd better watch out,

He's coming for you,

And he's bringing along,

A Santa or two,

The Santas are all coming for you.

You created the list,

Of naughty and nice,

Which makes you as bad,

So, you'd better think twice,

The Santas are all coming for you.

They'll kill you when you're sleeping,

They'll torture when you wake,

They'll hunt you down cos you're not good,

You have made a big mistake.

The Eve of Christmas

By Gemma Owen-Kendall

It hardly ever snowed on Christmas Eve in England especially on the coastal town of Cleethorpes, however mother nature decided to grant us all an early gift for a white Christmas. As there was no school due to the winter break I had the chance to go and explore the area all covered in white, there had been a good six inches of snow that'd fallen from the early hours of the morning. My parents had left yesterday to go visit my grandparents, but I chose to stay at home to look after our pet dog, Hunnie. She was a Staffordshire bull terrier, just vaguely a puppy with light golden brown fur with a white fur chest. Before my parents left, my mother gave me a couple of dos and don'ts round the house, although I was seventeen she still treated me like a child.

"Also Eve. Last of all, no parties." She told me before they were on their way.

Today I was taking Hunnie on my little adventure out into the snow, this was the first time she had ever stepped foot on the white ice cold substance. Wrapping up warm in my Ugg boots and thick woollen coat, I had put on a little doggy coat for Hunnie too, we made our way towards the seafront. The snow had stopped falling by the time we headed outside, along Cambridge street up to the promenade area. There were hardly any moving cars on the road, nature had taken its cause to blanket the roads over. Anyone who'd tried to drive in this weather, they were stuck on the intact snow along the edges of the road. As I walked by the street, I noticed the welcoming light of the Globe Coffee shop, I thought to myself that I would head there after our little walk.

As we reached the barrier to the sea wall, the clouds decided to open and let the thick snowdrops fall again only this time they were twice as thick. The wind blew strongly along with the fallen snow, I tried to look down at Hunnie who was struggling to walk through the elements. I picked her up and moved us quickly as

I could towards the Globe. The owner had spotted us approaching through the big open window and kindly opened the front door for me before I got there.

"Are you both alright?" the owner kindly asked me.

I nodded at him through shivering teeth and sitting down at a large vintage table. The owner was called Matthew, he was such a kind and welcoming gentleman. Through his spectacles, he always had friendly and caring eyes, for each customer. He placed a menu down in front of me.

"You are my first customer today, take your time, get warm and I will be back over soon to collect your order."

I gazed through each word on the menu deciding what to have, I felt the heating round the room soothe my cold muscles, as I gradually got warm I removed my coat, gloves, and hat. Hunnie was good as gold and just laid on the floor rolled up into a ball then eventually into a snore as she drifted off to sleep. The heat was then interrupted as the front door flew open and entered what I thought was a snowman. Whoever it was brushed the snow off himself to reveal one of the cutest guys I went to school with. It was Adam, I had a crush on him since we started school together those few years ago. The weather was really coming down thick and fast. Adam acknowledged me and sat down at the far side of my table.

"If it carries on like this, you might be stuck in here for the rest of the day," I heard Matthew call to us from behind the counter.

I just giggled at his comment but I sort of hoped that would not happen as I wanted to be back home in my nice warm house. I did not live too far away, but the weather looked dreadful and not safe to be heading back home. I gazed out of the window and in such a short space of time the snow blizzard had completely covered the majority of the glass frame.

"Don't worry I have a spare room upstairs you can all stay in." he kindly offered to us.

"Thank you." I smiled gratefully to him

Adam had now warmed up, so he gradually started to remove his coat, gloves and beanie hat and looked down at the menu.

"I'm going to have the New York pancake stack with a luxury hot chocolate." I mentioned to him. His eyes then moved up to look at me and he smiled.

"That sounds good, I am going to have the same."

Matthew had heard us so he went away into the kitchen area to prepare our orders, during this time I had a little catch up with Adam. it had been over a week since I last saw him at school and during our final period together we had a brief moment in English. During the class, we were discussing what Christmas and the festive season meant to us, Adam was sat next to me and I felt him gently touch my left hand. I looked round at him and he whispered softly into my ear 'Have a wonderful Christmas Eve. I will miss you.' I was touched by his gentle and caring words, these had stayed with me the past week playing that moment over and over in my head. Now the spirit of Christmas had granted me an early wish which was to see him again.

"I am so glad you are here." I said to him.

"Me too." He took my right hand into his. "I have not stopped thinking about you since we finished school."

This was my eve of Christmas to remember forever.

Festive Cheer.

By Ants Ambridge.

Christ, I'm fucked. If you asked any sane person if they'd like to only work one day in a year, they'd shake their heads faster than a nodding dog in a car with broken suspension. But it isn't all it's cracked up to be. I mean, yeah, I get 364 days off per year, apart from those twatting leap years that rob me of a day's rest. But I need that time off, this one night's work is usually the equivalent of about twenty years. Magic and all that good stuff. I can't explain how it works, I'm not Steven Hawking. Suffice to say, I put in more graft in one night than many people do their entire lives.

In case you haven't figured it out yet, I know there are some slow fuckers out there, I'm Santa. Saint Nicholas. Jolly old Saint Nick. Right now, the only jolly thing about me is the prospect that I'm just over half-way through this sodding shift. You must pardon my language, but

I'm fucked-in-half drunk from almost three quarters of a gallon of brandy. I swear a good portion of them mince pies had liquor in them too. I wish people would vary these treats up a bit. An evening of gorging on mince pies leaves me backed up for a week afterwards. Let me put it this way; I think I have an idea of how painful childbirth is.

I'm taking a wee break. I'm sat on top of Trump Tower with my legs dangling over the edge, appreciating the view of New York. I suppose it's a perk of the job I get to see so much of the world once per year. In my time off, there is no travelling, I'm confined to the small, sovereign nation of Grotto. Lights flick on and off in the distance and I can make out small faces pressed against the windows hoping to catch a glimpse of me on my rounds. Good luck with that kids; tonight, I'm invisible, otherwise I'd have to stop to listen to every request, take photographs and all that other shite that delays me no end. I learned that lesson the hard way.

The air is crisp, at least up here anyway. New York smells like piss, mostly on street level. It kind of does up here too, but that's because I pissed up here. I rarely urinate outside, I'm not an animal. But it's Trump Tower, and, Y'know, fuck that guy. Wearily, I stagger to my feet and command the reindeer to drop their foul payload atop the building too. I'm sniggering at how juvenile and petty I can be. Maybe it's the brandy. I flop into the sleigh and shout "Onwards Dancer! Onwards Prancer! Onwards…" Bollocks. I've forgotten their names again. "Just go, all of you!" One of them turns at looks at me with disdain. Aye, keep that up and I'll turn you into venison, you red-nosed bastard!

So, I steam through most of the night, uneventfully. There's less to do nowadays, kids are way too cynical these days. They just ask their parents for stuff. Suits me fine, it's not like I get paid for this anyway, not counting all the sickly sweet confectionary and booze. It's no wonder I'm so fat. Every year, I vow to exercise and use the cross fit trainer for ten minutes a day for a week, tops. Not this year though, I'll stick to it. Deffo. Anyway, soon my evening's toil will end, but I'm facing a new problem.

This isn't a one-man operation, far from it. There're the elves. Hardworking, diligent, efficient, but a bit simple. They work the entire year, unlike me. They seem happy with having food and a roof over their heads. It's not slavery... well, it sort of is, but they are free to leave if they like. I'm sure the pointy-eared little cretins could find gainful employment in panto's and shopping malls, but they are kind of insular. They like to keep to their own. Shit, I'm sounding like a bloody racist. I'm not. It's just how they are. The elves.

There's a flip side to their work ethic. Christmas Eve comes, and they get two weeks off (I'm not a monster). These little fuckers LOVE a piss up. Whilst I'm out distributing the fruits of their labours, they are drinking almost a lake-full of berry wine. Have you ever been confronted by an army of pissed-up, leery little elves? It's an experience. I guarantee at least five of them will say they quit and call me a fat fascist. I've just got to take it on the chin, let them blow off steam. If I retaliate, then I'd have an uprising on my hands. Bugger, I'm sounding like a deep-south plantation owner again. I'm not like that!

Every year; the same situation. Whilst I'm out delivering gifts harder than a piece-work driver, those little buggers are becoming raucously belligerent. A mini riot sparks off in the workshop most years as they squabble over this and that. Their tiny fists fly towards each other with malice. And let's face it, they are three-foot-tall each, they have very little power behind each blow. They get knackered far before anyone gets more than a scrape or a bruise. Whilst their squeaky voices are squawking threats and proclamations of hate, none of the dense bastards ever think to use the woodworking tools lying about. Told you they were simple. A chisel will have your ear off if you use the fucker right.

That isn't the worst part. And remember while all this shit is going on, I'm trying to get some fucking kip after work too. The violence ends and they carry on drinking. The next stage is the make-up sing song. Tuneless fucking dirges, like a bunch of strangled rodents. If you played an Alvin and the Chipmunks LP and flicked the speeds rapidly–you'd get the idea. It's awful and led me to an attempt to soundproof the workshop a couple of decades ago. Not only did it do very little to help, but the foam is very absorbent and the third stage of their celebrations doesn't lend itself well to the walls being covered with that type of material.

The more astute among you might have guessed what that third stage is. What do most couple do after they make-up? Yep. Angry, violent sex. Hatefucking I believe is the parlance of our times. They get the horn, big time. It's like a klaxon sounds in all their dopey little heads and they just drop their clothes and start banging. The ratio of male and female elves is skewed in favour of the males, so, well, they're forced to share. Doesn't seem to bother the Elve-ettes. They lay on their backs, all holes filled with hard Elven cock, with looks of joy in their eyes as they squeak with pleasure. A cacophony of Elf orgasms is an even more torturous sound than their frigging singing. This orgy last three days as they mix and match partners, like a coke-fuelled wife swap party.

Naturally, the party ends and as my hangover fades, theirs begins. They can't even look at each other for a few days afterwards–and rightly so. Dirty little fuckers. The entire workshop is awash with Elf sexual fluids. It smells like a shrimp factory, or worse, certain districts of London. This is where I am forced to crack the whip. That was a poor choice of phrasing, they are not slaves! But I have to make them clean up the milm and jism coating the floors, walls and crevices of the workshop. Therefore, I soon ripped out the soundproofing foam. Ever wondered why stocks in Air Wick rise in January? The place stinks. We go through a gross of those canisters, plug-ins and the like, to get the building smelling habitable again.

I'm shuddering at the prospect of it again. Perhaps this year I will film it? There must be a market for that somewhere. Worth a thought; I might be able to retire.

Acknowledgements

First, we would like to thank you readers for the taking the time to read this anthology, we hope you enjoyed each story and poem.

Second, a massive thank you to Matthew Head who owns the Globe in Cleethorpes. Without his coffee shop our writers group would not have continued and grown to how it has today. This book is dedicated to Matthew.

Third, thank you to all the story writers and poets who have took their time to come up with something for this anthology, without you all *Christmas Gifts* would not have happened.

Other Work by our Authors

Writer and author Gemma Owen-Kendall has the following short stories in these must-read anthologies:

Him and The Old Barge -   Monday At Six

The Text Message and Who Am I? - Fish And Freaks

Writer and author Ants Ambridge has the following must read novels currently on sale:

The Night Out

Backbones

GY Til I Die

Under The Unfamiliar Moon: Ten Tale Of Retribution

Leaving - Fish And Freaks

Soon to be released by Ants:

Tab Ends

Writer and author David Bromley has the following short stories:

The Purr-fect Murder and Above The Salt -   Monday At Six

Writer and Poet Kate Brumby has the following book on sale full of inspiring poetry:

In The Palm Of His Hand

Soon to be released by Kate:

His Guiding Hand

Writer and Poet Andy Richards has the following poetry collection on sale:

A Little Book of Randomness (under the alias of Lord Stabdagger)

You can find all these books on sale through Amazon.

Printed in Great Britain
by Amazon

32592741R00099